Open for Debate
National Health Care

Marshall Cavendish
Benchmark
New York

This book is dedicated to my husband, Michael Meissner.

The author gratefully thanks the following people
for sharing their insights and comments:
Greg D'Angelo, the Heritage Foundation;
Karen Davenport and Meredith King, Center for American Progress;
Ann H.; Roger Hickey, Campaign for America's Future;
Mike M.; James Watson, Mountain States Health Alliance.

Marshall Cavendish Benchmark
99 White Plains Road.
Tarrytown, NY 10591-5502
www.marshallcavendish.us

Copyright © 2009 by Marshall Cavendish Corporation

All rights reserved. No part of this book may be reproduced or utilized in any form
or by any means electronic or mechanical, including photocopying, recording, or by any
information storage and retrieval system, without permission from the copyright holders.

All websites were available and accurate when this book was sent to press.

Library of Congress Cataloging-in-Publication Data
Kowalski, Kathiann M., 1955-
National health care / by Kathiann M. Kowalski.
p. cm. — (Open for debate)
Includes bibliographical references and index.
ISBN 978-0-7614-2943-2
1. National health services—United States—Juvenile literature.
2. Insurance, Health—United States—Juvenile literature. 3. Medical policy—
United States—Juvenile literature. I. Title. II. Series.

RA395.A3K69 2009
362.1—dc22

2007027749

Photo research by Lindsay Aveilhe and Linda Sykes/Linda Sykes Picture Research, Inc.,
Hilton Head, SC.
The photographs in this book are used by permission and through the courtesy of:
Images.com/Corbis: cover; Yang Liu/Corbis: 6; Phototake/Alamy; 14; AP Photo: 18, 25, 64, 84, 107,
118; Brooks Kraft/Corbis: 31; Ed Kashi/Corbis: 37; Collection of the New-York Historical Sociey/
The Bridgeman Art Library: 43; Corbis: 51; Wally McNamee/Corbis: 60; Chip Surnodevilla/
Getty Images: 70; UPI photo/Laura Embry/Landov: 94; Mark Wilson/Getty Images: 115.

Publisher: Michelle Bisson
Art Director: Anahid Hamparian
Series Designer: Sonia Chaghatzbanian

Printed in Malaysia

1 3 5 6 4 2

Contents

1	**An Ailing System**	7
2	**Condition Critical**	23
3	**America's Medical History**	42
4	**Healthy Competition?**	63
5	**Universal Health Care: A Major Medical Makeover**	83
6	**Prognosis for the Future**	101
	Notes	122
	Further Information	140
	Bibliography	142
	Index	151

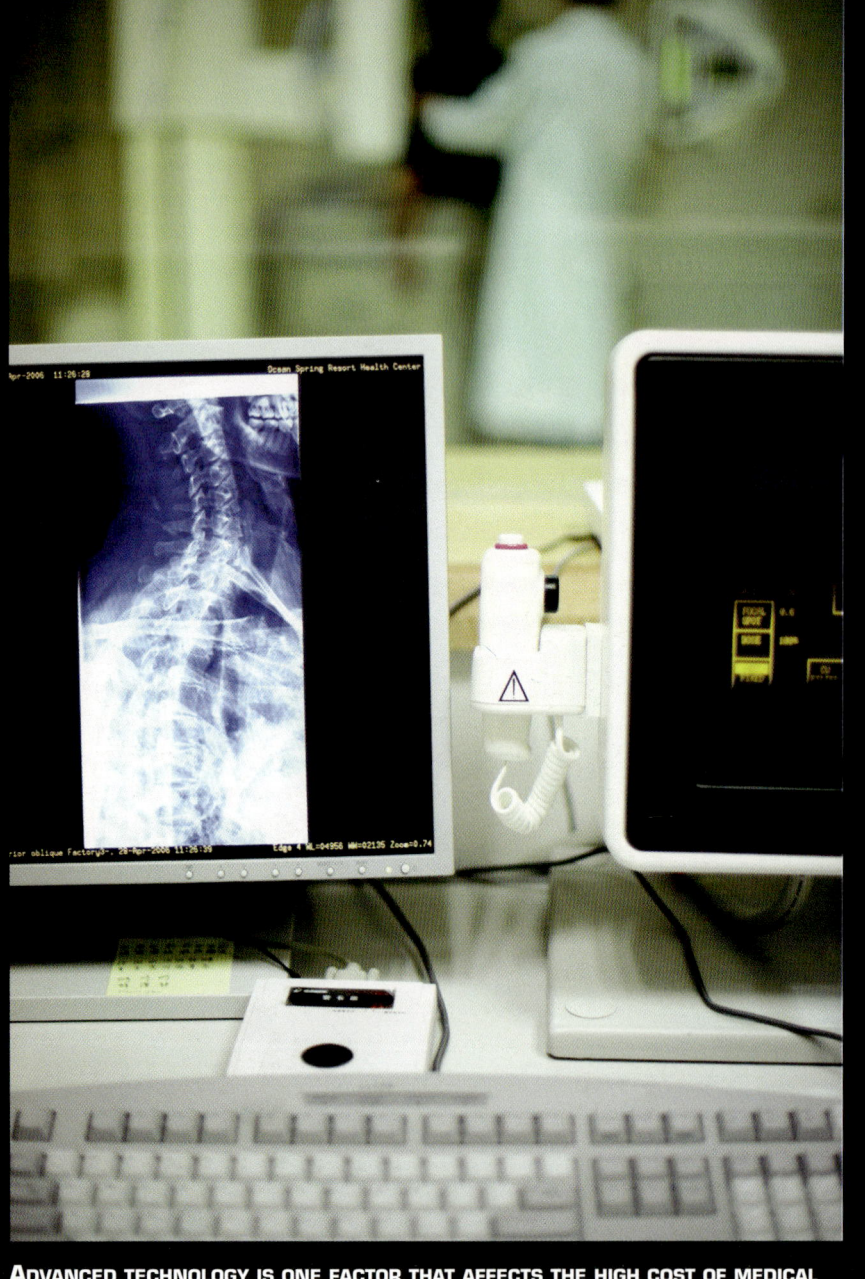

ADVANCED TECHNOLOGY IS ONE FACTOR THAT AFFECTS THE HIGH COST OF MEDICAL CARE. HERE, A FLAT PANEL COMPUTER MONITOR DISPLAYS A DIGITAL X-RAY IMAGE OF PART OF A PATIENT'S BODY.

1
An Ailing System

After Joey Palmer's motorcycle crashed into a guardrail, an ambulance rushed him to San Francisco General Hospital. Fortunately, Palmer had only bruised muscles and a fractured rib and could go home after several hours. Unfortunately, his hospital charges came to $11,082, including fees for X-rays and a CT scan—an imaging technique that produces detailed cross-sectional views of body areas. Doctors' fees added another $922.

Palmer could not pay those bills. Employed as a woodworker, he was one of approximately 47 million Americans without health insurance. An administrator eventually cut $4,569 from the charges. However, Palmer still owed more than $7,000.

"I'm not a bum, but I'm not making a lot of money right now," Palmer told the *San Francisco Chronicle*. "How is anyone supposed to pay a bill like that?" Palmer's injuries were minor, and he was otherwise generally healthy.

Alicia Facchino was confined to a wheelchair by multiple sclerosis. With no health insurance, Facchino could not afford long-term care as her health deteriorated. Her ex-husband helped with some procedures when he checked in on their school-age children. The children cleaned house and cared for their mother the rest of the time. Facchino's illness placed a strain on the whole family: physically, financially, and emotionally.

Bob Barton of Grafton, Massachusetts, had health insurance, but it was little help when he needed treatment for Dupuytren's contracture, an incurable condition that curls the fingers up like claws. With treatment, patients can use their hands longer.

Barton's doctor recommended a twenty-minute procedure called needle fasciotomy. Although European doctors had performed it for decades, the procedure was relatively new in the United States. Barton's insurer, Blue Cross Blue Shield of Massachusetts, balked.

The out-of-state doctor and surgical facility recommended by Barton's primary care physician were not on the insurer's approved list. The insurer also said the needle fasciotomy was not the "standard of care." In other words, it was not the usual procedure performed by health care providers in Barton's area for his condition. Ironically, the insurer would have paid for invasive surgery, which was riskier and cost $20,000.

For more than a year, Barton wrestled with insurance appeals and denials. Finally, in 2006, he spent $1,500 of his own money to have the needle fasciotomy done on his right hand. By the next day, he was back at work and using the hand.

A year later, Barton wanted the procedure performed on his other hand. Yet again Blue Cross Blue Shield would pay only for the risky, expensive surgery or nothing. "Why doesn't it make sense for them to give me what's necessary to fix my hand, especially when it's so much cheaper?" Barton asked.

An Ailing System

Tales like these are not isolated horror stories. Millions of people are faced with the uncertainty and costs that come from not having health insurance. Others have coverage but struggle to pay their share of the premiums and other health costs. Still others wrestle with getting timely payment for costs that should be covered.

Social reformers have called for drastic changes to America's health care system for almost one hundred years. Now policy makers are again calling for health care reform. They say the situation is more critical than ever.

A Complicated System

Before considering what is wrong with the system, it helps to have an overview of how things generally "work." About 250 million people, or 84 percent of the U.S. population, have health insurance. Most people insured by private plans get coverage through their or a family member's employer. Presently, about 61 percent of employers offer health care coverage.

Usually, employers pay a part of workers' health insurance costs. Employees pay the rest. The employers' share is generally tax deductible as a cost of doing business. Employees are not taxed on that share either, since they do not get the cash as income.

Nevertheless, rising costs of insurance increase employers' expenses. Thus, employers prefer to keep health care costs lower, whenever possible. Many employers contract with an insurance company, health maintenance organization (HMO), or both to offer coverage to their employees.

Premiums cover the insurer's expected payouts for a set policy period, based on statistical risks and prevailing costs, plus the insurer's costs for running the program and its profit. Generally speaking, the healthier the group of insured people, the lower their overall risks and the lower their insurance premiums. If the makeup of a group changes, or if more people than expected become ill, the risk of higher payouts increases. As a result, an insurer may raise premiums when the next policy period comes up. At that time, employers may make different choices about what plans to offer and what share they will pay.

Some companies fund health plans with their own money, plus employees' payments. These arrangements are called self-insured plans. Often a private insurance company or HMO will run such a self-funded plan under a contract with the employer.

Under a self-funded plan, the employer's fund pays all covered health care costs. Because federal law exempts self-funded plans from state insurance regulations and taxation, many large companies self-insure to take advantage of those benefits. Often, those companies reinsure some of the risks through a stop-loss policy. Such a policy protects against the risk that payouts under the employer's plan will be much higher than expected. In effect, it backs up the company's plan and protects the company against catastrophic loss. Otherwise, the company absorbs any costs that are higher than expected.

As a practical matter, employers' choices limit workers' health insurance options. Workers generally go with whatever programs the employer offers, as long as the employer pays a share. Although formats and programs vary, the main benefit is that they provide some financial protection from health care costs. Unless specifically stated otherwise, discussions about employer-provided insurance generally refer to any possible arrangements.

People who do not get health insurance through a job may buy policies on their own. As a general rule, such policies cost more than people pay when coverage is available through a job. Individuals do not have the bargaining power that employers do.

Also, workplace insurance plans spread risks over a

An Ailing System

group. Individuals generally cannot achieve this without joining another group that offers health insurance, such as a professional or trade association. Also, individuals who buy private health insurance policies pay the whole bill.

Millions of other people get health care as part of a government program. Medicare provides benefits to millions of people over age sixty-five. Medicaid and other programs provide health care for qualified people with low incomes. The Department of Veterans Affairs provides benefits to people who have served in the armed forces and use its hospitals and facilities.

For the most part, insurance pays costs that policyholders incur when they or family members get sick or hurt. However, programs generally require policyholders to follow specific rules to request payment. For example, health care providers or patients must submit claims in a certain way. Many other rules are part of insurers' managed care programs. Under managed care, insurers try to control costs.

For example, doctors often must be within a certain group, called a network. In an HMO, the network consists of the physicians who work for or contract with the organization. For other plans, physicians sometimes agree with an insurer in advance on the rates for their services. Seeing a specialist often requires a referral from an individual's regular, or primary care, physician. Going outside the network typically requires prior approval from the insurer, based on a showing of medical need. Patients who consult specialists or go outside the network may incur extra costs.

Some procedures must be approved to qualify for payment. One aim of preapproval policies is to cut down on surgeries, diagnostic tests, or other procedures that may not be medically necessary. Another goal is to steer patients toward less expensive treatments.

Policies have upper limits on how much insurers will

pay. Policies may also have exclusions that say the insurer will not pay for particular health problems. These limitations let the insurer control its potential financial exposure.

Also, many policies exclude preexisting conditions. These are health problems a person had before he or she got health insurance. The insurer's rationale is that its policies protect against risks that may or may not occur. From its standpoint, preexisting conditions are already known liabilities.

Even when insurance covers health care expenses, patients often must spend a certain amount of their own money before insurance pays anything. This amount is called a deductible. In recent years, high-deductible policies have become more common. Under their terms, policyholders may spend $1,000 or more before insurance pays anything.

In most cases, patients must also pay a certain amount per event, called a copayment. This may be a percentage of the total charge, or a set dollar amount, such as thirty dollars for each visit to a doctor's office.

Some health care providers require patients to pay first and then seek reimbursement from the insurer. More commonly, health care providers submit bills directly to patients' insurers. This arrangement lets patients avoid the hassles of extra paperwork and cash-flow problems.

In many cases, however, patients remain liable for charges if insurers do not pay. When insurers take weeks or months to pay claims, providers may send "past due" notices to patients, who in turn feel frustrated or harassed.

Meanwhile, health care providers spend significant amounts of time and money pursuing payment. Ultimately, they factor those costs into their fees. Health care charges also reflect other costs of doing business. Those costs include equipment costs and maintenance, facility costs, reg-

An Ailing System

ulatory compliance, and employee wages and benefits.

Health care providers also generally buy malpractice insurance. Malpractice is the failure of a professional person or facility to provide the appropriate standard of care. Medical malpractice insurance pays defense costs and legal judgments in case something goes wrong and a patient sues. Costs for those premiums are built into provider charges too.

Beyond all this, health care costs can vary, depending upon patients' insurance coverage. For a typical appendectomy, a hospital might accept about $6,200 from a private insurance plan and $4,900 for someone in Medicare. However, the same facility might charge more than $8,100 to someone with no insurance. If the person is poor, the facility could cut the price to around $1,800.

Patients like Alicia Facchino may go without some types of care. Yet health care providers also provide some services without payment. For example, nonprofit hospitals provide emergency care without regard to ability to pay and regardless of whether patients have insurance. Facilities generally do this to qualify for tax exemptions. Providing such care may also be a condition for receiving certain public funds or satisfying other legal requirements. For-profit hospitals are subject to less stringent restrictions and can more easily turn patients away.

In 2004 hospitals shouldered more than $25 billion worth of services that were not paid by patients or their insurers. Such services drive up health care providers' overall costs. Facilities often pass these costs along to other patients in the form of higher charges.

Facilities cannot always pass costs along, however. Sometimes the amount of uncompensated care grows high enough to jeopardize an institution's financial condition. After charity care shot up 70 percent in one year, a hospital in Albany, New York, faced a $4 million budget

National Health Care

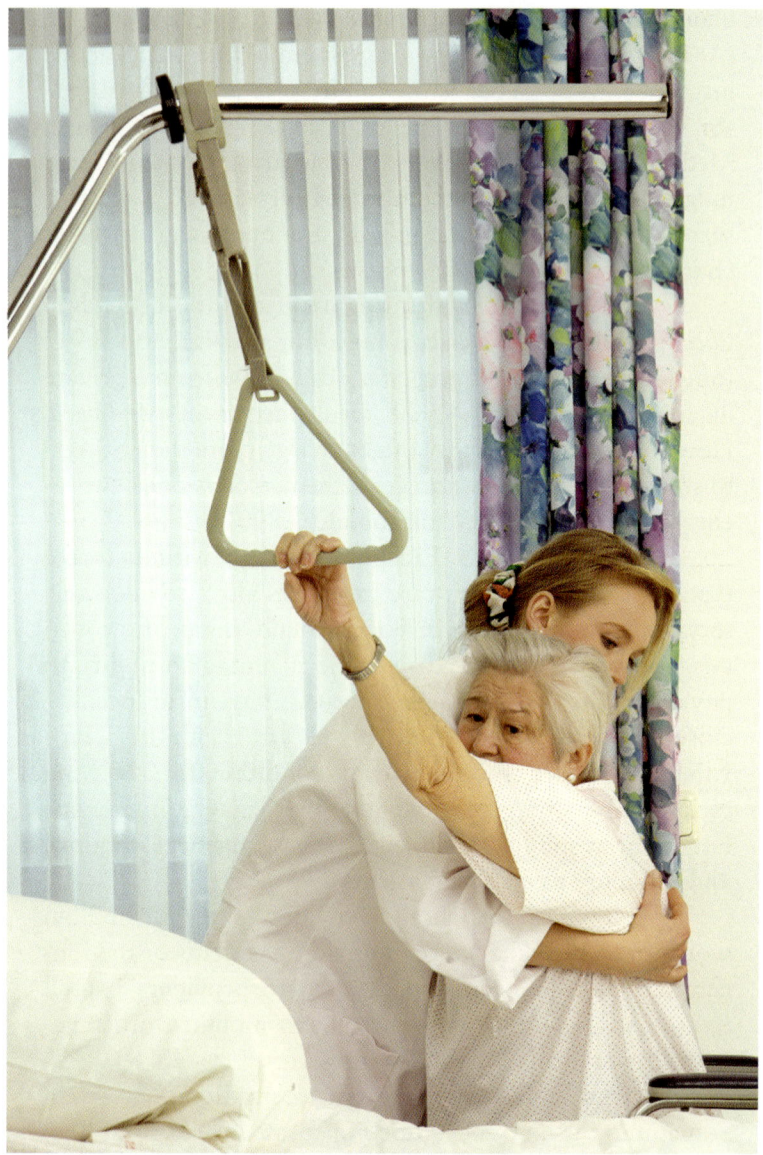

THIS NURSE HELPS AN ELDERLY WOMAN OUT OF HER WHEELCHAIR. THE FEDERAL MEDICARE PROGRAM PROVIDES BASIC MEDICAL COVERAGE FOR AMERICANS WHO ARE SIXTY-FIVE AND OLDER.

An Ailing System

shortfall. Prince George's Hospital in Cheverly, Maryland, narrowly avoided closing down in 2007, but its financial outlook remained bleak. Half of its patients were uninsured, and it had mounting debts and cash flow problems.

Many hospitals have merged with other health care providers in order to stay afloat. Twenty-five years ago, many cities had dozens of independent hospitals. Now facilities in those cities may be part of two or three systems controlled by larger umbrella organizations. Around Cleveland, Ohio, most private hospitals are part of the Cleveland Clinic or University Hospitals' systems. MetroHealth System, which is a public health care provider, serves the area too.

Despite difficulties, health care is a huge industry in the United States. The country spends more than $2 trillion a year on health care. In 2005 that equaled 16 percent of America's gross domestic product, or GDP. (The GDP is the total of goods and services produced by a country.) On a per capita basis, the $2 trillion figure came to $6,697 per person—more than any other nation in the world.

However, the United States does not lead the world when it comes to the overall quality of its health care system. Healthy-Adjusted Life Expectancy (HALE) is a country's average total life expectancy minus years of expected ill health or disability. The HALE for the United States ranked 20 out of 30 among the nations in the Organisation for Economic Co-operation and Development (OECD). Among the same OECD countries, the United States also had the highest obesity rate and the third highest infant mortality rate. On a global level, the infant mortality rate for the United States exceeded that of thirty-six other countries, including Cuba and Croatia.

Also, in a survey of twenty-two OECD countries, the United States had the third highest rate for deaths from misadventures, or mistakes, during surgical and medical

National Health Care

care. Moreover, the United States was the only developed country that did not guarantee access to a base level of health care for all its citizens. Such data signal little improvement since 2000, when the World Health Organization ranked the U.S. health system only thirty-seventh among 191 countries.

Certainly some Americans receive first-rate care from some of the finest hospitals and physicians in the world. Meanwhile, millions of Americans settle for less. The Commonwealth Fund graded the U.S. health care system on categories such as length and quality of life, access to care, efficiency, and nearly three dozen other indicators. The United States got an overall score of 66 out of a possible 100.

In fact, the 47 million people who have no health insurance at all comprise roughly 16 percent of the population, or one-seventh of all people in the United States. Another 16 million adults are underinsured, which means that they have some health insurance but cannot pay their health expenses without hardship.

Most uninsured people live in homes with at least one working family member. Some people go without insurance for part of a year as a result of changing jobs or losing jobs. Up to one-third of the population had gaps in insurance coverage, or periods during the past two years of going without coverage.

In short, the United States is not getting top value for its health care spending. The situation seems to be getting worse, too. From 2000 to 2007, premiums for employment-based health insurance—the most common type of private insurance in the United States—jumped more than 80 percent. Employees' share of premium payments was more than $1,000 higher than it was in 2000.

Families are not getting the same value, either. Out-of-pocket spending for copayments, deductibles, and noncovered items has risen. Insurers have scaled back coverage. Meanwhile health care costs continue to spiral. The Department of Health and Human Services foresees that by 2016, health care spending could rise to $4.1 trillion.

A Call for Action

By 2007, a majority of Americans were calling for government action on health care. President George W. Bush stressed health care policy in his 2007 State of the Union address. Candidates for the 2008 presidential election pushed other proposals for health care reform.

Some plans are new and innovative. Other ideas have been around for more than half a century. Yet many Americans feel that the need to find a workable solution to the national health care crisis is more pressing than ever.

As the national debate goes on, several states have already enacted or proposed their own health care reforms. Starting in 2005, Maine's DirigoChoice program began offering health care to individuals and small businesses. Subsidies from the state make the premiums more affordable. For example, instead of paying $1,500 monthly for a private Blue Cross policy, individuals could buy coverage through Dirigo for just $200 per month. (*Dirigo*, Maine's motto, means "I lead" in Latin.)

In less than two years, Maine's program brought the state's percentage of uninsured people down from 14.5 to 12.5 percent. Even with financial help, though, some lower income people do not buy health insurance because they believe it is too costly.

Massachusetts and Vermont both enacted "personal responsibility" programs. Everyone who drives needs a driver's license, and everyone who goes to school needs certain immunizations. By the same reasoning, these two states' laws require everyone to carry basic health insur-

National Health Care

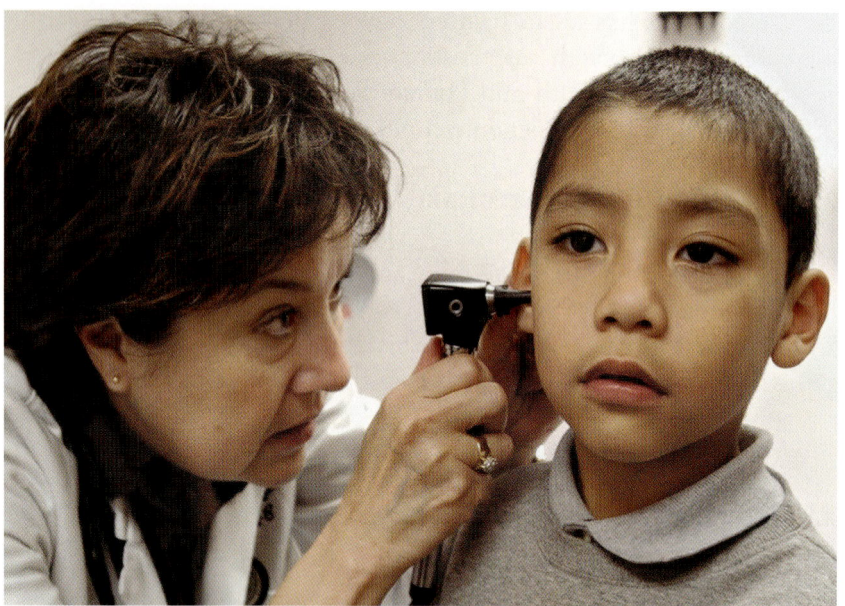

THIS DOCTOR EXAMINES A CHILD'S EAR AT A MEDICAL CLINIC IN SACRAMENTO, CALIFORNIA. THE STATE'S MEDICAID PROGRAM COVERED THE CHILD'S MEDICAL COSTS AT THE CLINIC, BUT NOT ALL DOCTORS ACCEPT MEDICAID PATIENTS.

ance. Individuals who do not comply could face higher tax liability. In theory, the penalty would make up for added costs to the state that result from uninsured people's failure to carry insurance.

Such initiatives set minimum requirements for insurance plans. In Massachusetts, for example, health insurance must include prescription drug coverage. Most people will likely get policies through their workplaces. When this is not possible, individuals and small businesses can get coverage through the Massachusetts' Connector program, which acts like a central market for a variety of plans. Low-income people can also get public assistance through programs such as Medicaid.

An Ailing System

Tennessee has adopted "mini-medical" health insurance coverage. The Cover TN program offers low-cost health insurance to small businesses and their workers for as little as $50 per month. Another program, Access TN, provides similar coverage to individuals who do not otherwise have insurance. Plans have no deductibles, and co-payments are low. However, the coverage limit for 2007 was just $25,000 per year, of which only $15,000 could be for hospital fees.

"In today's medical market, it doesn't take a long time to use $25,000," admitted James Watson of Mountain States Health Alliance, a hospital system that accepts Cover TN. "But the premiums are really low." The program is optional, and individuals and businesses can stay with conventional health care policies with higher limits for catastrophic events.

Maryland's Fair Share Health Care Fund Act called on companies with more than 10,000 employees to spend at least 8 percent of their payroll on workers' health care coverage or else pay into a state fund. However, a federal appeals court overturned the law in 2007. Because of a federal law regulating employee benefits plans, the state could not force companies to offer certain benefits. Also, the legislative history showed that state lawmakers improperly meant to target one large employer, Wal-Mart.

Universal health insurance has also become a hot topic in Connecticut, Pennsylvania, Oregon, Missouri, Hawaii, Minnesota, and elsewhere. Different proposals are likely to face strong debate. Even when bills pass, the ruling on the Maryland plan signals that court challenges are likely. If that happened, any action on certain types of health care reform might have to occur at the federal level. However, it is not clear whether any proposed laws would pass.

If it were easy to fix America's health care system, presumably lawmakers would have made any necessary

Crisis in California

One in five Californians has no health insurance at all, and millions more are underinsured. Lawmakers' responses represent a range of policy choices.

Senate Bill 840, passed by the California legislature in 2006, would have set up a single-payer health care system. Sponsored by state senator Sheila James Kuehl, a Democrat, the bill would have replaced private health insurers with a statewide trust. Both employers and workers would have contributed to that trust, which would have paid everyone's health care expenses. No one could be turned down, and individuals would remain free to use either private or public health care providers. Although the Republican governor vetoed the bill, the state senate passed the same plan again in 2007.

Meanwhile, Governor Arnold Schwarzenegger presented his own health care plan. Anyone who refused to get coverage through an employer or otherwise could face higher taxes or garnishment (withholding of some of the person's wages). Businesses with ten or more workers would have to offer health insurance or pay 4 percent of payroll into a state fund. Lower income people could use that fund to help buy their own insurance.

Insurance companies, for their part, could not refuse coverage on the grounds of age or preexisting conditions. Schwarzenegger's plan would also force companies to spend at least 85 percent of revenues on health benefits, which would limit administrative costs and profits for shareholders. Doctors and hospitals would have to pay more taxes, although they would get greater reimbursements from state-run programs.

The proposal left leeway for different types of coverage, including high-deductible and so-called bare bones plans. However, all people would have some type of insurance. "Everyone ends up with a better deal," said Schwarzenegger.

California lawmakers Don Perata and Fabian Núñez (both Democrats) proposed another health care plan that would not force individuals to have insurance. However, employers would have to spend at least 7.5 percent of their payroll on health care. As with Schwarzenegger's plan, employers would either offer health care coverage to workers or pay into a government fund. However, the Democrats' plan called for more comprehensive benefits.

National Health Care

changes by now. However, different groups have had strong interests in maintaining the status quo. As with most policy matters, the question of who pays is also a major issue.

As you read, consider the conflicts between what would be desirable and what is achievable in the real world. Think about the goals of fairness, justice, and equal opportunity. Then factor in competing interests of various camps.

The United States was founded on the idea that all people have a right to life, liberty, and the pursuit of happiness. Ideally, that concept would include living a healthy life, with access to quality care at an affordable price. America as a country must decide whether that ideal is worth the costs, and if so, how to pursue it.

2
Condition Critical

The United States has debated about health care for decades, but the issue is more critical now than ever. Record numbers of people go without health insurance, and medical costs keep skyrocketing. At the same time, economic and social issues make people who do have insurance feel more insecure than ever.

Living Longer

The good news is that Americans are living longer than earlier generations. Thanks to antibiotics and other drugs, infections that once led to high death rates are now mostly curable. New surgical procedures and diagnostic methods have helped find and treat cancer, coronary disease, and other serious ailments. Medical breakthroughs have played a huge role, too.

As one result, people are living longer with chronic conditions that sometimes require significant medical intervention. Even when conditions are under control, patients can require expensive medications for years.

National Health Care

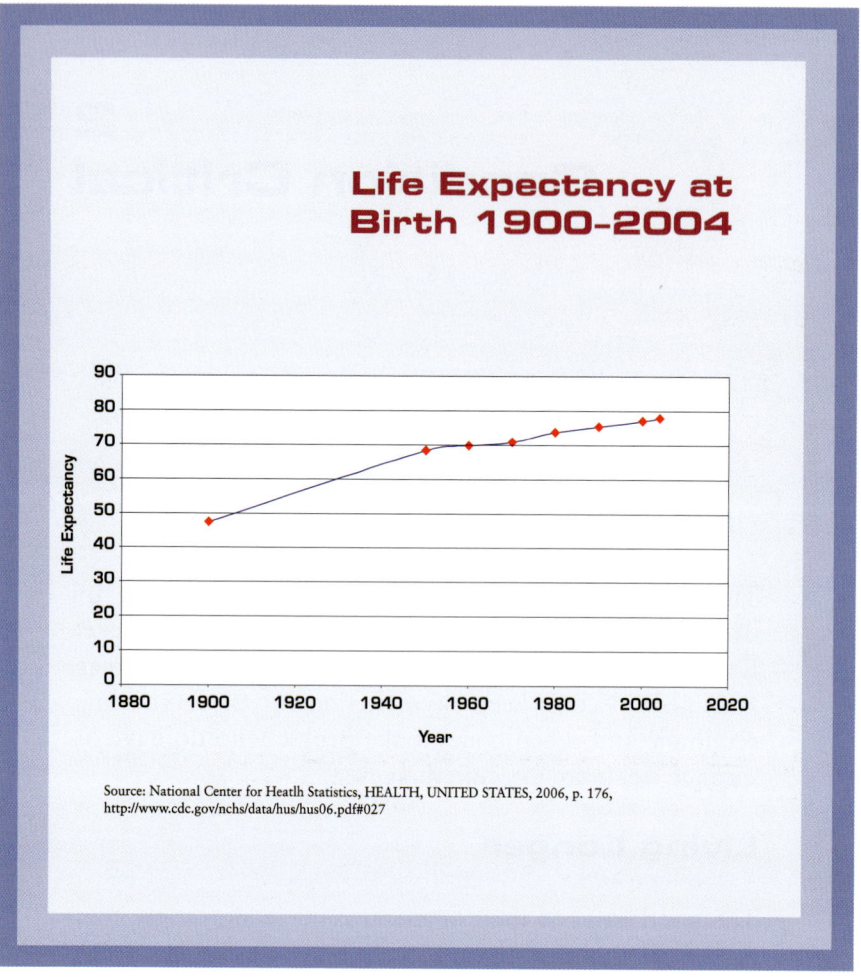

For example, nearly 21 million Americans—7 percent of the population—have diabetes, and many of them require insulin and blood-testing supplies on an ongoing basis. They are also more likely to have complications from other illnesses or injuries. Asthma affects approximately 20 million Americans. Patients often need anti-

Condition Critical

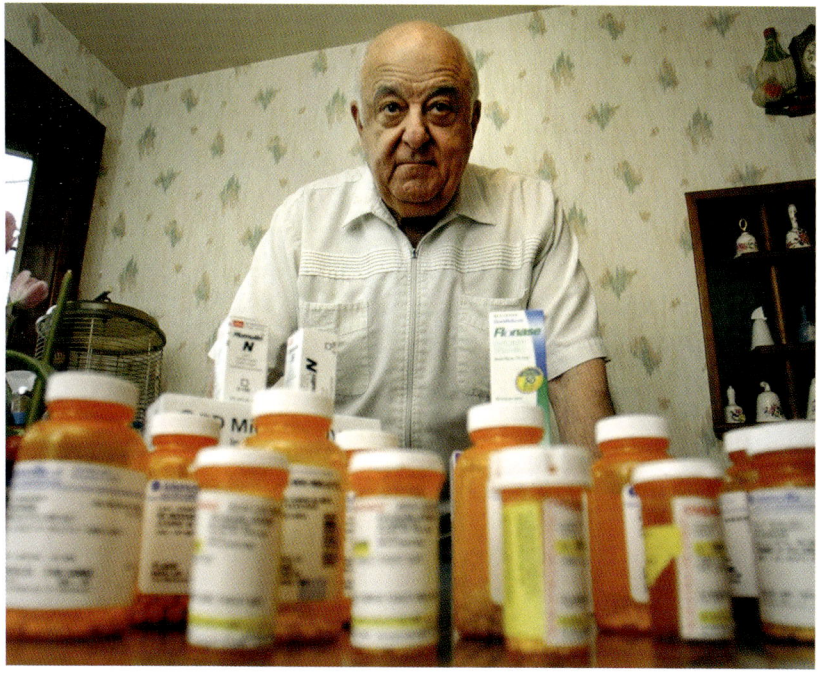

PRESCRIPTION MEDICINE COSTS CAN PLACE A BIG BURDEN ON PATIENTS AND THEIR FAMILIES. EVEN WITH BENEFITS FROM A STATE DISCOUNT DRUG PROGRAM, THIS ELDERLY MAN AND HIS WIFE MUST SPEND MORE THAN $2,000 PER YEAR FOR THEIR MEDICINES.

inflammatory and other drugs to control symptoms, as well as rescue medicines for emergencies.

Cardiovascular disease numbers are even higher. About 72 million American adults have high blood pressure. About 105 million adults have high cholesterol levels. High blood pressure and high cholesterol can cause heart attacks, strokes, and other problems. Although some patients do not need active intervention, millions must take medicines regularly to control blood pressure and cholesterol, to reduce their risks of more serious problems.

The list goes on. Many patients with chronic conditions can lead normal lives by following a proper treatment regime. Yet that costs money.

Other conditions such as multiple sclerosis, HIV, or muscular dystrophy can devastate patients' lives, as well as family finances. For cancer, a year's medicines can run from $50,000 to $100,000. Surgery, radiation therapy, and other treatments drive costs much higher.

In short, we may expect to live longer than previous generations. However, we can also expect to have substantial medical needs over the long term.

Rising Costs

In 1997 the cost for an average five-day hospital stay was more than $11,000. By 2004, the average stay was down to 4.6 days. However, the mean costs had soared to $20,455.

Physicians' fees add another chunk to medical costs, especially if patients must see multiple doctors. While insurance arrangements may place some limits on what physicians charge, fees can still be thousands of dollars. Like people in other businesses, doctors need to cover costs for equipment, offices, staff, and their own insurance, with enough left over to support their families. Many physicians also carry significant debt from student loans, which adds to financial pressure.

As in many other areas of modern life, health care today relies heavily on advanced technology. Hi-tech scans can often identify medical problems more quickly and cheaply than exploratory surgery. Such scans have saved many patients' lives by detecting disease at an early, more treatable stage. Minimally invasive surgery results in faster healing times and fewer complications for patients. Other advanced procedures and treatments extend lives and improve the quality of living beyond the expectations of anyone even a few decades ago.

However, such technological wonders come at a cost. For example, magnetic resonance imaging (MRI) scans can pinpoint diseased or damaged tissue. Each scan typically costs from $500 to more than $1,000. Part of the charge covers staff costs for conducting and interpreting the MRI, as well as films and related supplies. The charge must also cover part of the facility's cost for the MRI equipment, which can easily exceed $1 million.

No single technology works for all cases, though. Positron-emission tomography and computerized tomography (PET/CT) scanners can help doctors tell whether chemotherapy is working for breast cancer patients. These imaging technologies also help patients with cardiac conditions, epilepsy, Alzheimer's, and other diseases. Equipment costs between $2 million and $4 million to buy and install. Charges per scan can exceed $1,500.

A left ventricular assist device, a type of mechanical heart, dramatically improved the last two years of Frank McMasters' life. The Idaho man could barely move before the operation, but afterward he was able to live a fairly normal life. Yet the procedure involved more than $200,000 in medical costs, including $70,000 for the device itself.

Complicated equipment is not the only thing with a big price tag. Stents, the tiny tubes that prop open clogged arteries, can cost from $1,000 to $3,000 each.

The OECD has noted that "use of expensive medical procedures explain[s] part of the differences in overall health-care spending" between the United States and other developed nations. Starting in the late 1990s, technological advances accounted for roughly half the growth in the United States' per capita health costs. High demand for advanced medical technology continues to push health care costs up.

Because of costs, insurers might pressure health care providers to meet higher standards in order for patients to have coverage for new technologies and drugs. On the other hand, various health care providers may feel competitive pressure to offer advanced technologies. Both doctors and medical facilities want the advantages that technology can give to patients. They also want to avoid potential charges of malpractice from those who might later claim that such technology should have been used.

For their part, patients want the best care for themselves and their families. Especially if insurance will pay, they want the benefits of advanced technology. For many patients and their families, cost is no object when a loved one's life is at stake.

Prescription Problems

Drug costs are another factor in the fight against higher medical costs. Patients do not shop for prescription drugs the way they buy frozen vegetables or trash bags. They purchase what their doctors prescribe. Often, patents still protect those brand-name drugs from competition.

When AARP studied 193 brand-name drugs in 2007, the senior advocacy group's researchers found that prices had gone up 6.2 percent in one year. That jump was nearly twice the 2006 inflation rate of 3.2 percent. The ten drugs with the greatest price increases had jumps of 13 to 30 percent. That group included common medicines for asthma, allergies, depression, and insomnia.

Families USA reported similar findings: a 9.2 percent increase for 2006 in prices for the fifteen drugs prescribed most often to senior citizens. A year's supply for one cholesterol-lowering medicine rose from $785.40 to $857.40.

Because of high prices, some consumers use Internet pharmacies. Others have taken "field trips" to buy cheaper medicines in Canada. In many cases, medicines are not approved for import into the United States. Also, the foreign pharmacies are not subject to regulation by the federal Food and Drug Administration.

Patent protection is one reason why drug companies can charge high prices. Patents give inventors the exclusive right to make products or license others to make them. In other words, the patent holder gets a monopoly for a set period of time, generally twenty years. In return, the patent holder must tell how the invention is made and works. The disclosure requirements broaden scientific knowledge.

The pharmaceutical industry says it needs patent protection to recover huge research and development costs. As Ken Johnson of the Pharmaceutical Research and Manufacturers of America (P*h*RMA) explains:

> **Medicines discovered by our industry require anywhere from 10 to 15 years of research and development and cost an average of nearly $1 billion; this innovation is critically important in the never-ending war against disease.**

Companies must also do extensive studies and trials to meet government rules in the United States and abroad. More than a dozen years can pass before a new drug gets to market. Only then can a company start recovering its costs.

"A large majority of the projects we embark upon fail," notes Steven Projan at Wyeth Pharmaceuticals. Nor does every approved drug become a commercial success. Pharmaceutical companies set prices to cover their overall research and development expenses, not just those for a particular drug. They need to make a profit if they are to stay in business. To finance additional research, companies want capital investments too. A good profit record helps attract stockholders and other investors.

Nevertheless, Representative Henry Waxman (D-CA)

National Health Care

and other politicians criticize drug companies' profit levels. During the first six months of 2006, profits for the ten largest manufacturers increased more than $8 billion above 2005 levels for the same period.

Americans spent a total of $252 billion on prescription drugs in 2005. Prices continued to rise in 2006, from about 5 percent for hospital settings to between 7 and 9 percent for retail drugstores. Drug spending was expected to increase anywhere from 4 to 16 percent in 2007, depending on where patients got their medicines.

Since 2000, even insured patients have had to pay significantly greater amounts for their medicines. Some plans have high deductibles, requiring patients to spend several hundred dollars before prescription drug coverage kicks in. Some policies also steer policyholders to a preferred online pharmacy. Even if e-mail is available, patients miss out on immediate answers from live pharmacists and cannot easily ask follow-up questions. Patients may also face delays and red tape in getting prescriptions filled.

Uninsured patients have been hit the hardest. Most of them have had to pay the full price for prescriptions. Moreover, while some large health plans have negotiated better prices, drug companies and pharmacies rarely charge the same lower prices to other customers.

Sensing customers' frustration, some companies, such as Target and Wal-Mart, have begun advertising low prices for various generic drugs. Yet retailers may still profit from generic drug sales. Or they may make up any amounts in the prices charged for brand-name drugs. Also, generic drugs are not an option for all patients. If physicians prescribe newer, brand-name medicines, patients cannot simply ask their pharmacists to substitute a cheaper drug.

The pharmaceutical industry has also begun a program to provide medicines to individuals who can prove financial need. "Help Is Here," the industry ads said. As

Condition Critical

PRESIDENT GEORGE W. BUSH TOUTS MEDICARE'S PRESCRIPTION DRUG BENEFIT PROGRAM AT A 2006 MEETING WITH SENIOR CITIZENS IN COCONUT CREEK, FLORIDA. WHILE THE PROGRAM'S SUPPORTERS SAY IT CREATES A HUGE SAVINGS FOR SENIORS, CRITICS CHARGE THAT THE BIGGEST BENEFITS GO TO PRIVATE DRUG COMPANIES.

of 2007, the program had helped over 3.6 million people. Yet that was still less than a tenth of the country's uninsured population.

In 2003 Congress passed a law establishing a Medicare prescription drug program. Senior citizens can buy low-cost Part D coverage, as it is called, through private insurance companies.

Part D coverage pays drug costs up to a certain amount. After that, seniors must pay for medicines out-of-pocket. Part D kicks in again if drug costs exceed another limit. The plan thus has a "donut hole." It covers people

Dealing for Better Drug Prices?

On April 18, 2007, the Senate killed a bill that would have let the federal government negotiate drug prices under Medicare Part D. The House of Representatives had already passed such a bill in January 2007.

"Negotiating the best price is the American way," argued Senator Debbie Stabenow (D-MI), who cosponsored the Senate bill. "This isn't rocket science. These kinds of negotiations occur in the private sector all the time, [and] occur in other government programs. . . ." The Veterans Administration, for example, routinely bargains for better drug prices.

Supporters said that the proposed law could save $28 billion to $30 billion per year. Democrats generally favored the bill, and they held a majority of seats in the Senate. Because the bill dealt with budget issues, though, Senate rules required 60 yes votes for passage. Thus, despite 55 votes in its favor, the bill did not pass.

"The Senate today chose access over restrictions, choice over government mandates, and competition over price controls," said Senator John Kyl (R-AZ), who had fought the bill. Interestingly, the Medicare Part D program drove much of the increase in drug companies' profits for the first part of 2006. Debate over the effects of Medicare Part D on drug company profits continues.

with relatively low costs and very high costs, but not those in the middle.

Medicare prescription coverage has been controversial from the start. The 2003 law forbade the federal government from bargaining with drug companies on prices. Other provisions called for strict financial scrutiny of the Medicare program in general. Questions about the program's financial health had been brewing since the 1990s.

In 2007, the Medicare program forecast that by 2019, it would be spending more than it received through taxes and other sources. By 2041, the program could run out of money. Of course, millions of seniors rely on the program for health care coverage. Both supporters and critics question how to deal with the program's financial future.

Meanwhile, the debate about health care coverage for the rest of the population has become more pressing. Medical care has been changing. Medical costs are up. And coverage from workplace health insurance is less reliable than many Americans once believed.

Jitters about the Job

As medical costs soar, people become more concerned about their ability to pay for health care. Because most people in the United States have health insurance through their own or a family member's job, reductions or loss of insurance coverage can result from changes in employment or family situations.

Laws passed in 1986 and 1996 help somewhat. Under the 1986 law, various people who lost health care coverage provided by an employer could continue the policy, at their own expense, for a limited time. The Health Insurance Portability and Accountability Act of 1996 let individuals purchase coverage in more situations. The 1996 law also limited insurers' ability to deny coverage for preexisting conditions to workers who changed jobs. Thus, if someone who had insurance through one job developed a medical condition, a job change would not automatically result in denial of coverage.

The laws went only so far, though. While people could choose to continue coverage under a former employer's health plan, the employer no longer had to contribute. Also, the laws limited how long former employees could retain coverage. Thus, insecurity about employment still translates into worries about health care coverage.

While jobs have always had turnover, many of today's grandparents spent a decade or more with the same employer. People whose job provided good health benefits could count on being able to pay whatever doctor or hospital bills might arise.

By 2006, Americans' median length of time for holding jobs was just about four years. (In any survey, half the values fall above the median, and half fall below it.) That number was not vastly different from the figures for the prior two decades. However, median tenure for workers aged 45 to 54 dropped more than two years from 1983 to 2006. For workers 55 to 64, the decrease was nearly three years.

Compared with younger groups of workers, people in these age groups are more likely to have children or dependent parents for whom they must pay heath care costs. Meanwhile, people in these age groups are starting to deal with their own age-related health issues. They also often have significant expenses for housing, children's college costs, and other obligations. For middle-aged workers especially, less overall job tenure means greater economic insecurity.

"Millions of Americans are just a pink slip away from losing their health insurance, and one serious illness away from losing all their savings," said President Bill Clinton in 1993. During the early 1990s, more than 4 million people lost health insurance coverage as a result of changing jobs. When they did get new jobs, weekly earnings averaged 20 percent less for men and about 25 percent less for women. Even if a new job provided health coverage, the worker's contribution consumed a higher share of wages. Meanwhile, the employee would struggle to pay the costs of food, clothing, and housing. Worries about job security and health insurance continued into the twenty-first century. Not everyone lost from a job change, and some people came out ahead. But the odds were against it.

A shift away from manufacturing explains part of the change. Formerly, someone with just a high school education could get higher wages in the manufacturing sector than in other jobs. In 2004 the United States had 5.2 million fewer manufacturing jobs than it had in 1979. The efficiency that comes from robotics, computers, and other new equipment often translates into a need for fewer workers.

Job losses extend beyond the manufacturing sector. Acquisitions and mergers have eliminated thousands of jobs. Others disappeared as a result of corporate reorganizations. From the 1980s to the mid–1990s, corporations slashed more than 4.5 million middle-management jobs.

The growing move toward globalization also accounts for job losses. In many cases, modern telecommunications and transportation make it relatively convenient for companies to base various operations overseas. Lower prevailing wages and less stringent regulations often allow cost savings as well.

Foreign competition puts pressure on operations within the United States. Companies that cannot keep up must downsize or close. Thus, wages and benefits rise more slowly. Alternatively, more people lose their jobs.

As a separate matter, lower-paying jobs are less likely to offer attractive health benefits. Barely two-thirds of workers earning less than ten dollars an hour worked for firms offering health insurance, one study found. However, nearly nine-tenths of workers earning more than fifteen dollars an hour could get coverage through their employers.

Many companies offer health benefits only to permanent employees who work full-time. In 2005, for example, Wal-Mart provided insurance to fewer than half its employees. Coverage went only to full-time employees with at least two years on the job.

As of 2006, 24.7 million people nationwide worked in part-time positions, compared to 119.7 million people holding full-time jobs. A majority of part-time workers probably could not get health insurance through their employers. Some may have shifted into part-time or temporary work after losing other jobs.

Likewise, some people work as independent contractors, which means that they do not get job benefits from others. As of 2005, 10.3 million people—about one of every thirteen American workers—fell into this category. Independent contractors are technically self-employed. They generally work for one or more companies—sometimes even for former employers. In years past, many companies hired full-time workers for jobs they now outsource. Unless the Internal Revenue Service challenges the arrangement, companies can thus avoid costs for Social Security, workers' compensation, and job benefits.

People who cannot get health insurance through an employer often seek it through other avenues. However, premiums for individual policies are generally higher than employer-provided coverage. In part, one loses the benefit of group rates, and of course, an employer is not picking up any costs. Beyond this, preexisting conditions can prevent people from getting affordable policies. Or, a particular policy may exclude coverage for some conditions altogether.

Condition Critical

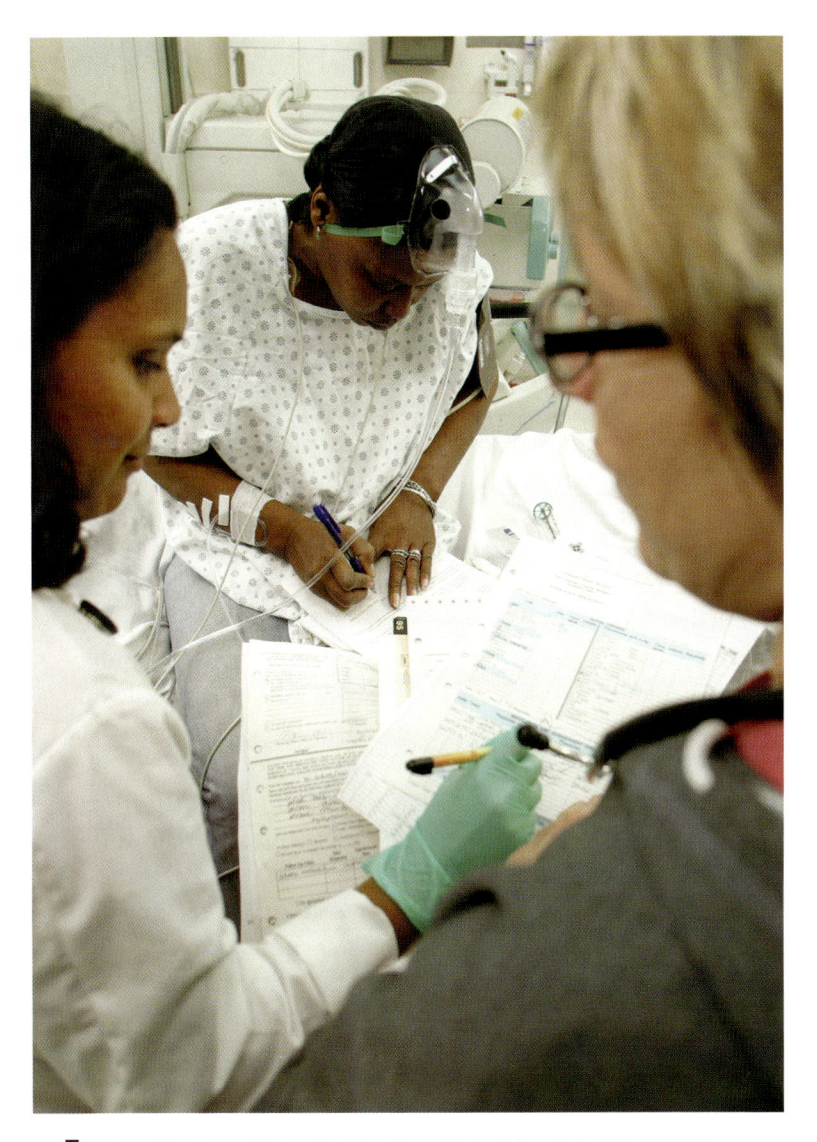

THIS ASTHMA PATIENT FILLS OUT PAPERWORK AT THE EMERGENCY ROOM OF A SAN FRANCISCO COUNTY HOSPITAL. EMERGENCY ROOMS ARE THE FIRST AND LAST RESORT FOR MOST OF THE 47 MILLION WHO ARE UNINSURED BECAUSE THESE UNITS AT PUBLIC AND PRIVATE NONPROFIT HOSPITALS GENERALLY TREAT EVERYONE WITHOUT REGARD TO ABILITY TO PAY. OTHERWISE, MOST HOSPITALS ARE FREE TO TURN AWAY THE UNINSURED—AND OFTEN DO SO.

Higher Prices, Less Coverage

Since the twenty-first century began, health insurance costs have risen at more than twice the rate of inflation. Overall, premiums increased 87 percent from 2000 to 2006.

Much of the increase comes from the dramatic rise in medical costs. For an insurer to stay in business, premiums must cover anticipated payouts, costs of administering the program, and expenses for offices, advertising, legal compliance, and other business-related matters. For-profit insurers also set premiums to allow a profit for shareholders who have invested money or other resources in the company.

Consequently, as medical costs have risen, so has the price of insurance coverage. In theory, health insurance spreads the risks of medical expenses among a company's policyholders. To determine how much to charge, companies generally consider a group's demographic profile and risks, its past experiences, and prevailing medical costs. For some covered patients, the insurer expects to pay out more than the premiums. That is all right as long as it pays out less than the premium amounts collected from other policyholders.

When payouts are higher than anticipated, however, insurers must raise premiums or lose money. Some policyholders merely pay the higher costs. Other healthier policyholders or their employers may seek coverage elsewhere. If those remaining in the plan are generally less healthy, the insurer will likely have higher payouts the following year. Then it may well raise premiums again.

In short, health insurance is a business, and businesses expect to make a profit. In return, insurers limit customers' financial exposure to potential medical expenses. But a company that cannot remain financially viable can no longer insure customers.

With recent rises in premium costs, many people feel a significant financial squeeze. According to the Kaiser Family Foundation, family coverage through employer-provided health insurance cost an average of $11,480 in 2006. Workers paid nearly $3,000 of that amount—85 percent more than their average share in 2000. Workers at companies with fewer than two hundred workers paid nearly $900 more for family coverage than those at larger businesses.

"Employers are trending more towards a higher cost share for employees," noted Tom Daschle, a former Senator who has since lobbied for health care reform through the Center for American Progress (CAP). "Employees are being asked to pay a lot more up-front costs."

As workers' out-of-pocket insurance costs rise, they become more likely to decline coverage offered at work. In one study, 22 percent of workers who were eligible for such insurance did not take it. In another study, 54 percent of uninsured people said that high costs prevented them from purchasing health insurance.

J. Edward Hill, former president of the American Medical Association (AMA), has observed that 40 percent of the uninsured people in the United States "choose to be uninsured." Some of those people may be irresponsible. Others, especially younger workers who enjoy good overall health, may fail to appreciate the importance of health insurance. Limited income may force other people to spend their money on things they see as more immediate needs.

If trends continue, the numbers of companies offering coverage could go down, while the number of uninsured people rises. As Jon Gabel at the Center for Studying Health System Change explains:

> **We are still losing the race between premiums and workers' earnings—and if that trend persists, em-**

National Health Care

ployer-based coverage will continue to decline as fewer employers and workers can afford the cost of coverage.

"All businesses are dealing with increased health care costs," notes Meena Seshamani, a CAP researcher who studied ten companies' health care programs in detail. Regardless of whether the companies were small, medium, or large, all wanted ways to keep costs in line.

Retiree coverage was usually the first area dropped, followed by cutbacks in dependent-care benefits. Various companies dropped eye care and dental programs as well. While higher deductibles and copayments help control policy premiums, they push up the total amount patients and their families pay out-of-pocket. In other words, companies and workers are paying more for health coverage. However, they are getting less for their money.

Few companies are happy about cutting back health benefits. However, higher health insurance costs hurt their competitiveness. Worker health care costs add about $1,500 to the price of a General Motors car sold in the United States. The prices of imported cars made in countries with government-funded health programs do not reflect those costs.

Such pressures led several large corporations to join with unions and nonprofit policy groups in the Better Health Care Together Campaign. Founding members included AT&T, Intel, Kelly Services, and Wal-Mart. The group wants national health care reform with universal coverage by 2012.

"[O]ur current system hurts America's competitiveness and leaves too many people uninsured," said Wal-Mart president and CEO Lee Scott. "Government alone won't and can't solve this crisis."

"Our WWII-vintage health care insurance system is

woefully out of step with the global economy," added Kelly Services president and CEO Carl Camden. "Workforce mobility and flexibility have been historic strengths of the American economy. Unless we act, and act soon, on health care reform, that competitive advantage will be at serious risk."

Health care reform is no longer just a social welfare issue. It matters to America's economic well-being too. Moreover, health care reform is no simple matter of "the people" versus "big business." Groups across a broad spectrum have a stake in the issue.

This does not mean that all companies agree with unions and other special-interest groups on what to do. Companies do not even agree among themselves on the best course. Nonetheless, the greater number of groups calling for reform increases the chances that lawmakers will take action. Yet the health care debate is not a new subject. As the next section details, policy makers have debated the topic for much of the last century.

3
America's Medical History

We have seen that most people with private insurance today get coverage through their employers. Public programs provide health care for millions more. Still other people get whatever insurance or other health care services they can afford on their own. Understanding how the United States got to this point calls for a review of the country's health history.

The "Next Great Step" in the Progressive Era?

When the twentieth century began, patients and their families paid medical bills from their own funds. Those who could not afford medical care might get services through doctors' goodwill or a few charitable organizations. Otherwise, they did without.

Meanwhile, many doctors practiced with scant training. Their treatments were often based more on superstition than science. Certainly, some doctors had good qualifications. Others practiced quack medicine to make a quick buck. In 1910 educator Abraham Flexner issued

America's Medical History

THE U.S. GOVERNMENT EXERCISED LITTLE REGULATION OVER MEDICINES DURING THE NINETEENTH CENTURY. PRODUCTS SUCH AS THESE WITH NO PROVEN MEDICINAL VALUE, BUT WHICH PROMISED TO CURE A VARIETY OF AILMENTS, WERE SOLD WITH SUCH CLAIMS UNCHALLENGED.

National Health Care

a detailed report on medical education. Flexner called for higher admissions standards, rigorous academic requirements, and a strong core curriculum. "The point now to aim at is the development of the requisite number of properly supported institutions and the speedy demise of all others," Flexner wrote.

As state licensing boards followed Flexner's advice, substandard medical schools closed. While 131 medical schools were operating in 1910, only 76 remained twenty years after the Flexner report. With less competition, doctors became more financially secure.

Meanwhile, America's population was growing. As the country became more industrialized, some politicians and policy makers pondered the problem of medical costs.

Germany had passed a law requiring health insurance for certain workers as early as 1883. That law had expanded by 1900 to include more groups. By 1911, several other countries were also considering or adopting their own health insurance laws. American reformers thought the time was ripe for action in the United States.

President Theodore Roosevelt had pushed for progressive reforms during his two terms in office. When his successor, William Howard Taft, failed to follow through on various programs, Roosevelt decided to challenge him in the next presidential election. Roosevelt lost the Republican Party nomination to Taft in 1912 and ran as a third-party candidate for the Progressive Party.

Roosevelt's 1912 platform called for widespread health insurance. Industry would pay part of the costs. The public could pay some part as well. In Roosevelt's view:

> **It is abnormal for any industry to throw back upon the community the human wreckage due to its wear and tear, and the hazards of sickness, accident, invalidism, involuntary unemployment, and**

old age should be provided for through insurance. This should be made a charge in whole or in part upon the industries, the employer, the employee, and perhaps the people at large to contribute severally in some degree.

Roosevelt and Taft lost the election to Woodrow Wilson. However, health insurance stayed on the political agenda. In 1916 the American Association for Labor Legislation (AALL) called for compulsory health insurance for all industrial workers earning less than $1,200 per year. Workers and employers would each pay 40 percent of the costs. Government would pay the remaining 20 percent.

"Health insurance will constitute the next great step in social legislation," predicted Rupert Blue, president of the AMA in 1916. The physicians' group believed that if such a plan were adopted, patients should remain free to choose their own doctors.

Although more than a dozen states considered bills based on the AALL proposal, none became law. Indeed, the AALL proposal faced strong opposition, even from labor leaders. American Federation of Labor (AFL) leader Samuel Gompers wanted workers to support unions, rather than trusting in the government's protection. "Compulsory or workers' sickness insurance is based upon the theory that they [the workers] are unable to look after their own interests and the State must interpose its authority," Gompers declared.

Commercial insurers and various businesses also resisted government-run health insurance. "A good, hard-headed business firm can do these things better than any form of state government," said D. R. Kennedy of the B. F. Goodrich Company.

America's entry into World War I postponed further discussion on health insurance laws. Afterward, in 1920 the AMA adopted a resolution opposing any compulsory health insurance. Its stance would stymie national health insurance proposals for decades.

From the Roaring Twenties to Deep Depression

As America's economy boomed during the Roaring Twenties, proposals for health insurance laws stayed in the background. Yet costs remained a concern. In 1927 eight foundations set up the Committee on the Costs of Medical Care (CCMC). Its fifty members included economists, sociologists, doctors, and public health experts.

When the CCMC published its recommendations in 1932, it supported group insurance:

> **The Committee recommends that the costs of medical care be placed on a group payment basis, through the use of insurance, through the use of taxation, or through the use of both these methods. This is not meant to preclude the continuation of medical service provided on an individual fee basis for those who prefer the present method.**

Optimally, people would pay for such insurance on reasonable terms. To the extent they could not, costs would be borne by the general public, based on the ability to pay.

By 1932, however, the United States was deep into the Great Depression. Nearly 25 percent of the country's work force had no jobs. Lawmakers were much more concerned with the economy than with health care.

Nonetheless, organized medicine made its objections clear. One concern was whether the doctor-patient relationship could really be protected once third-party payers got involved. Another was whether public funding for medicine would lead to heavy government regulation of doctors. Morris Fishbein, editor of *JAMA: The Journal of the American Medical Association*, railed against the forces that he believed were behind the CCMC's recommendations: "public health officialdom [and] social theory—even socialism and communism." Throughout his years of leadership, Fishbein argued that any form of national health insurance worked against the core values of American society. Many physicians agreed with him. And when a group of 430 doctors tried to push for a national health plan in 1937, the AMA publicly scolded them for "careless participation in propaganda."

Meanwhile, President Franklin D. Roosevelt had asked his Committee on Economic Security to consider national health insurance. After extensive lobbying by the medical profession, though, Roosevelt decided not to release the committee's report.

Faced with opposition, Roosevelt decided that it was more urgent to ensure a minimum income for the nation's elderly people. That program, Social Security, would be funded by taxes collected from people who were younger and working. Additionally, the Roosevelt administration set up a small aid program for poor mothers and children.

Supporters of broad health coverage did not give up. For example, Senator Robert Wagner (D-NY) and others tried to get national health bills passed several times during Roosevelt's four terms. Strong opposition from Republican politicians and organized medicine doomed their efforts to failure.

Group Plans Grow

Meanwhile, health care providers were also feeling the crunch of the Depression. From their viewpoint, a steady income seemed better than sporadic payments, or none at all. Starting in 1929, Baylor University pioneered a plan for people to "prepay" for hospital care. The American

Hospital Association later approved of such plans and persuaded Congress to exempt them from state insurance regulations. Thus, Blue Cross was born.

Blue Shield began similar plans in the 1940s to pay fees for doctors within their networks. The Internal Revenue Service treated Blue Cross and Blue Shield as nonprofit organizations. As a result, they did not pay federal income tax. As another advantage, many states exempted the plans from their insurance rules. One rationale for the exemptions was that the risk pool for each plan was the whole community, rather than an individual company's employees. Whether this distinction should have made a difference is unclear, but it helped Blue Cross and Blue Shield grow.

Prepaid group practice plans also got their start during the Great Depression. An Oklahoma farmers' group had sponsored the first such plan in 1929. Similar plans sprang up elsewhere. At Desert Center, California, Sidney Garfield offered medical care to laborers working on an aqueduct to bring water from the Colorado River to Los Angeles. The cost was ten cents per day.

Several years later, industrialist Henry Kaiser was heading up construction of the Grand Coulee Dam in Washington. In 1938 Kaiser arranged with Garfield to provide medical care for the dam's 10,000 workers and their families. Kaiser's company paid seven cents per day for adults and, when children were added, twenty-five cents per week for them.

When World War II broke out, Kaiser shifted to shipbuilding in California. He and Garfield continued offering prepaid health services for workers and families. After the war, a nonprofit plan began offering such services to the general public. The company would grow into Kaiser Permanente. Such prepaid plans were the forerunners of today's health maintenance organizations, or HMOs.

For a long time the AMA had opposed group medical

practices and prepaid care by physicians. One fear was that the AMA's sole practitioners would be at a disadvantage if they had to compete with groups and prepaid plans. In some places, such as the District of Columbia, the AMA barred physicians in group practices from joining its local chapter and urged hospitals to deny them privileges. In 1943 the Supreme Court ruled that the AMA's actions in Washington had been unlawful. That paved the way for further growth of group practices.

America's labor movement also grew substantially from the 1920s to the 1940s. Labor and management interests negotiated the first employment contract with group health benefits back in 1926. By 1942, just over three dozen insurance companies offered group health insurance policies.

Wage and price freezes during World War II became a major force behind the growth of employment-based insurance. Because of the war, qualified workers were in short supply. Companies could not offer higher take-home pay, so more employers began offering health benefits. Companies deducted premiums as a business expense. Employees did not pay income tax on premiums, either.

The number of insurers offering health plans grew. By 1951, 77 million people were covered in some sort of health plan. By 1960, almost 70 percent of America's full-time workers had some health benefits.

Thus, health benefits became linked to employment. Even though most Americans with private health insurance got it through their or family members' jobs, some interest in a national health insurance plan remained.

Truman Takes a Stand

On November 19, 1945, Harry S. Truman became the first president to propose health care for all Americans. Truman's five-part plan included building new hospitals, expanding programs for mothers and children, and funding more medical research. Most important, Truman wanted universal coverage for health care costs. He also supported disability payments to make up for lost income owing to sickness or injuries.

In a novel move, Truman stressed preventive care, especially for children. "The health of American children, like their education, should be recognized as a definite public responsibility," declared Truman. "In the conquest of many diseases, prevention is even more important than cure."

Political conservatives strongly opposed the expanded role of government and the taxes that Truman's plan would require. Organized medicine, led by the AMA's Morris Fishbein, felt threatened as well.

The AMA launched a massive media blitz. Ads aired on 16,000 radio stations and appeared in 10,000 newspapers. Public opinion polls had initially showed support for Truman's plan. But that support could not survive the AMA's rhetoric about "socialized medicine."

After all, Truman's proposals came at the start of the Cold War—open hostility just short of war between the United States and its allies, on the one hand, and communist countries, on the other. To support "socialized medicine" would have been un-American.

Congress did fund new hospital construction. Thanks to the Hill-Burton Hospital Survey and Construction Act of 1946, new hospitals sprang up in many rural areas. However, Truman's plan for national health insurance died.

Medicare Makes Its Debut

By the 1960s, the political winds had changed. President Lyndon Baines Johnson committed the country to a "war on poverty." That included health care needs for two of society's most vulnerable groups: the elderly and the children of the poor.

"Inadequate hospital care is an indecent penalty to place on old age," Johnson declared in 1964. If Americans would pay an average of $1 per month over their working lives, he said, "all Americans can face the autumn of life with dignity and security."

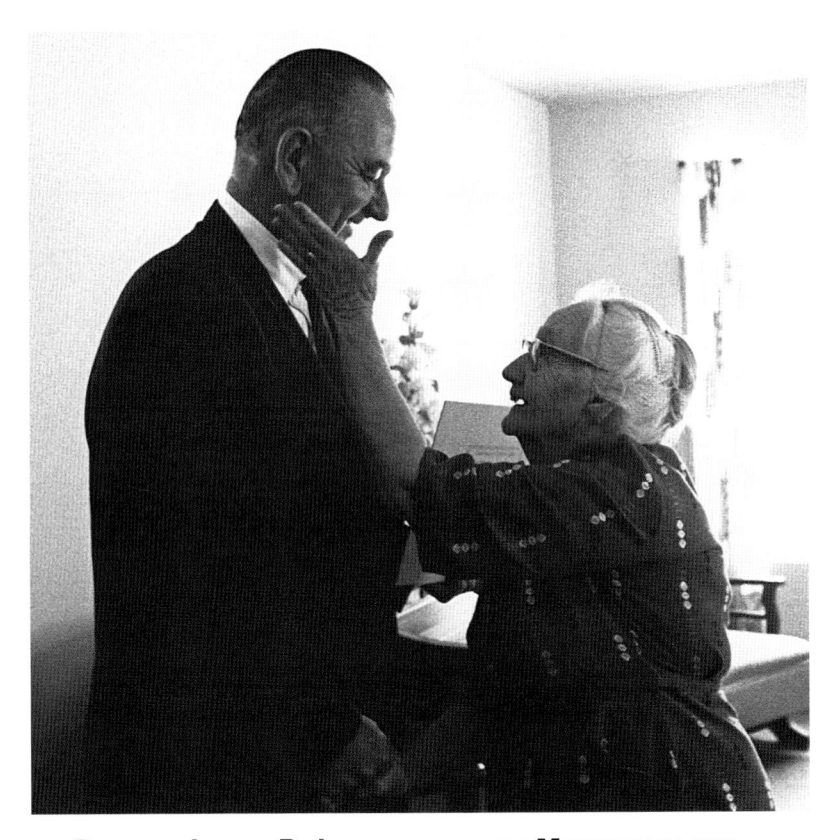

PRESIDENT LYNDON B. JOHNSON SIGNED THE MEDICARE BILL INTO LAW IN APRIL 1965. THIS PROGRAM ESTABLISHED A BASIC HEALTH INSURANCE PROGRAM FOR AMERICANS AGED SIXTY-FIVE AND OLDER, WHICH MADE AT LEAST ONE ELDERLY WOMAN GRATEFUL ENOUGH TO THANK HIM IN PERSON.

President Truman Proposes National Health Care

President Harry Truman's national health care plan included a bold proposal to provide universal health insurance for all Americans. Excerpts from his November 19, 1945, address to Congress follow.

> We should resolve now that the health of this Nation is a national concern; that financial barriers in the way of attaining health shall be removed; that the health of all its citizens deserves the help of all the Nation. . . .
>
> I recommend solving the basic problem by distributing the costs through expansion of our existing compulsory social insurance system. This is not socialized medicine. . . .
>
> A system of required prepayment would not only spread the costs of medical care, it would also prevent much serious disease. Since medical bills would be paid by the insurance fund, doctors would more often be consulted when the first signs of disease occur instead

of when the disease has become serious. Modern hospital, specialist and laboratory services, as needed, would also become available to all, and would improve the quality and adequacy of care. . . .

The ability of our people to pay for adequate medical care will be increased if, while they are well, they pay regularly into a common health fund, instead of paying sporadically and unevenly when they are sick. This health fund should be built up nationally, in order to establish the broadest and most stable basis for spreading the costs of illness, and to assure adequate financial support for doctors and hospitals everywhere. . . .

None of this is really new. The American people are the most insurance-minded people in the world. They will not be frightened off from health insurance because some people have misnamed it "socialized medicine" . . . .

Socialized medicine means that all doctors work as employees of government. The American people want no such system. No such system is here proposed.

Under the plan I suggest, our people would continue to get medical and hospital services just as they do now—on the basis of their own voluntary decisions and choices. Our doctors and hospitals would continue to deal with disease with the same professional freedom as now. There would, however, be this all-important difference: whether or not patients get the services they need would not depend on how much they can afford to pay at the time. . . .

We are a rich nation and can afford many things. But ill-health which can be prevented or cured is one thing we cannot afford.

National Health Care

Leaders in organized medicine and political conservatives had successfully fought prior proposals. Promises not to interfere with fees charged by hospitals or doctors lessened some of the AMA's objections.

More important, strong interest groups got behind the proposed programs. While the AFL had objected to the AALL's plan four decades earlier, labor unions now solidly supported the idea of government-sponsored health programs. Many people were finding that their pensions did not provide enough to cover hospital or doctor costs after retirement.

The elderly were another group whose political clout grew during the early 1960s. In 1958 former high school principal Ethel Andrus had founded the American Association for Retired Persons, now known as AARP. Then as now, the group lobbied hard for health care coverage.

Together, retired people and union members held considerable voting power. Awareness of these voting blocs, plus extensive lobbying, persuaded Congress to create Medicare and Medicaid in 1965. To honor the elderly former president, Johnson signed the bill into law in Truman's hometown of Independence, Missouri.

Medicare provided health coverage for almost all people over age sixty-five. Part A would pay for a set number of days at a hospital or, after 1967, a skilled nursing facility (nursing home). Part B let people buy optional low-cost coverage for doctors' fees or other non-hospital-based services. The initial charge was just $3 per month.

Like Social Security, Medicare is an entitlement program. In other words, almost everyone qualifies just by reaching the age of sixty-five. In contrast, Medicaid is a needs-based program. Only those whose income falls below a certain income level and meet other conditions can receive Medicaid benefits.

Medicaid offers medical coverage to poor children and

their caretakers, as well as blind and disabled people with low incomes. The federal government makes grants to states. States then run their own programs, with varying levels of benefits. By 1982, all fifty states offered Medicaid.

Spiraling Costs in the 1970s and 1980s

Health care was also a priority for Johnson's successor, President Richard Nixon. In less than a dozen years, America's health care spending had nearly tripled, from about $27 billion in 1960 to $75 billion in 1971. "Yet, despite this huge national outlay," Nixon told Congress, "millions of citizens do not have adequate access to health care."

In Nixon's view, much of the spending increase was due to price inflation. Thus, Nixon aimed "to encourage sensible economies—in the use of health facilities, in direct cost control procedures, and through more efficient ways to bring health care to people at the community level."

HMOs seemed to offer an answer. Generally, HMOs fared better financially if fewer participants got sick or injured. Preventive measures would cost HMOs money up front. Yet HMOs encouraged such steps because, in the long run, their members' collective health care costs would be lower. People taking preventive measures would lead healthier lives, too.

The Health Maintenance Organization Act of 1973 gave a big boost to HMOs. An HMO that met the law's requirements was exempt from various state insurance regulations. It could qualify for government grants and loans. More importantly, employers offering health benefits had to offer an HMO option along with any other plan.

National Health Care

U.S. Health Care Spending 1960–2005

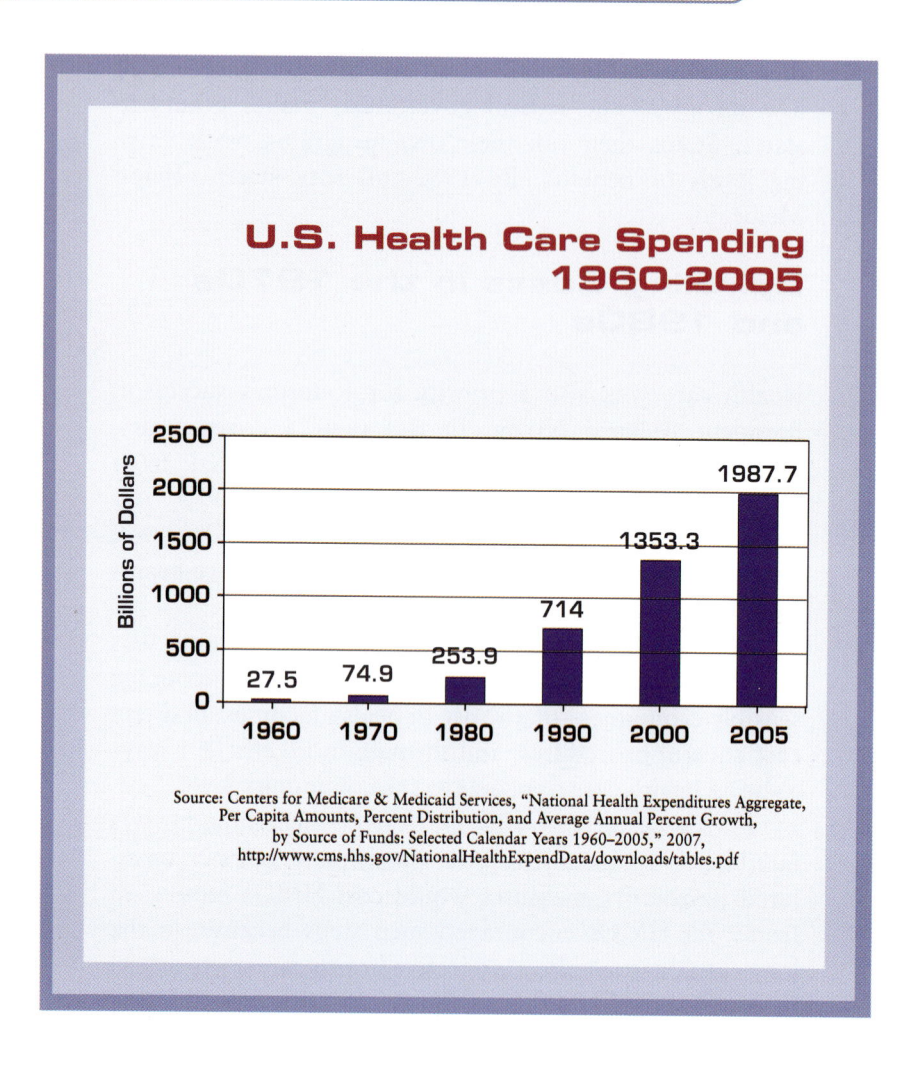

Year	Billions of Dollars
1960	27.5
1970	74.9
1980	253.9
1990	714
2000	1353.3
2005	1987.7

Source: Centers for Medicare & Medicaid Services, "National Health Expenditures Aggregate, Per Capita Amounts, Percent Distribution, and Average Annual Percent Growth, by Source of Funds: Selected Calendar Years 1960–2005," 2007, http://www.cms.hhs.gov/NationalHealthExpendData/downloads/tables.pdf

In theory, lower costs would give HMOs a competitive advantage over other health care providers. In turn, policy makers hoped, competition would keep overall medical costs down.

Nixon also wanted to close gaps in insurance coverage. His proposed National Health Insurance Standards

Act called for virtually all employers to provide minimum health insurance coverage for employees. Workers would choose between standard fee-for-service arrangements or membership in HMOs. Those who were self-employed or others who did not qualify for employer-provided plans could buy coverage at group rates through plans run by individual states.

For low-income people, Nixon proposed a government-funded family health insurance plan. The plan would assume responsibility for part of the group already covered by Medicaid and expand on it.

At the same time, Nixon wanted to rein in Medicare and Medicaid costs. Among other things, Medicare would not pay for certain hospital costs if the institution's building projects had not been authorized by a regional planning agency. For Medicaid, Nixon proposed changing the federal government's share and offering incentives for states to use HMOs for Medicaid patients.

Meanwhile, Senator Edward Kennedy (D-MA) and Representative Martha Griffiths (D-MI) proposed alternative legislation. Their idea was to provide universal health coverage through a government-run social insurance plan. Nationwide budget planning, the sponsors said, would control overall spending.

Neither Nixon's proposal nor Kennedy's plan passed, although Congress did pass pro-HMO legislation in 1973. In 1974 Nixon proposed a plan called the Comprehensive Health Insurance Program. As before, health insurance for most people would come through employers, rather than being paid for out of taxes. Kennedy then offered a new proposal similar in structure to Nixon's. However, it called for workers to pay less of the costs.

Organized labor balked at both plans. Nixon's plan for workplace-based coverage did not apply to everyone, and workers might have to shoulder a significant share of

National Health Care

the premiums. Kennedy's plan imposed fewer burdens on workers and provided more benefits. Yet labor leaders did not think it went far enough. In the end, Congress passed neither plan.

Soon after Nixon's resignation in 1974, Congress passed the Employee Retirement Income Security Act, known as ERISA. In general, ERISA set minimum standards for employer pension plans. States could not regulate plans that met those standards. States likewise could not regulate health benefit plans if employers self-insured. Employers could save money if they funded their own health benefit plans instead of relying on outside insurers.

As a result of the legal changes made by ERISA, many large companies chose to self-insure. Often, they contracted with HMOs or insurers to administer the programs. That would lead to later conflicts over malpractice and other issues. Otherwise, President Gerald Ford made no significant changes in America's health policy.

A few months after he took office in 1977, President Jimmy Carter proposed legislation to limit hospital price increases. Carter also wanted expanded health screening for children in low-income families. His most ambitious proposal was a National Health Plan, under which no family would have to pay more than $2,500 per year for medical expenses. That limit would protect against catastrophic illnesses that could rack up crippling debts. Yet the plan fell short of being a full-scale program for all medical costs.

Carter countered his critics by saying, "[N]o child of poverty, no elderly American, no middle-class family has yet benefited from a rigid and unswerving commitment to this principle of all or nothing." Nevertheless, Congress failed to pass Carter's plan.

Neither of the next two presidents, Ronald Reagan and George Herbert Walker Bush, pushed for major health care reform. Meanwhile, within the health insurance market, supporters of managed care were gaining influence. Insurers, HMOs, and others tried to control costs by limiting when and how patients could obtain expensive treatments. Requirements often frustrated patients and physicians, however. And despite managed care, health care costs continued to grow.

Clinton's Health Security Plan

Bill Clinton promised health care reform when he ran for president in 1992. Soon after he took office, Clinton's wife, Hillary, headed a task force on health care reform. In September of 1993, the president presented the group's ideas to Congress.

Under the Clinton plan, every American would have a health security card guaranteeing benefits that could "never be taken away, health care that is always there." Health plans could not refuse coverage for preexisting conditions or drop patients with high claims.

Comprehensive coverage would include emergency care, hospital care, doctor visits, and diagnostic services. Benefits would cover treatment for mental health and substance abuse problems. They would also include preventive care.

As in the current system, most Americans would get health insurance through their employers, but the new proposal called for a choice of at least three plans. Anyone not covered by an employer's plan would purchase policies themselves or get government assistance. All plans would use a single claim form, versus the 1,500 different forms in use then.

"There cannot be any such thing as a free ride…," Clinton said. "[E]very employer and every individual will be asked to contribute something to health care." Small

National Health Care

President Bill Clinton and First Lady Hillary Rodham Clinton attend a conference to promote their 1993 health care plan. The Clinton plan promised all Americans that they would have health care that's "always there"—but it did not make it through Congress.

businesses would get discounts. Larger employers would pay extra. Health insurance premiums for self-employed people would be tax-deductible expenses.

To keep costs under control, plans would borrow concepts from managed care. Meanwhile, the government would cut waste and inefficiency in the Medicare and Medicaid programs. Cost savings there could offset government subsidies under the health security plan.

The public's initial response to Clinton's speech was generally positive. People had questions, but a majority supported the program. They liked the idea of health insurance coverage "that can never be taken away."

America's Medical History

Paying for the plan proved to be a sore point. Some people objected to the requirement that employers pay up to 80 percent of health insurance premiums. An extra payroll tax on large employers was also controversial, along with a proposed cigarette tax of up to a dollar per pack. And while the president predicted that cost savings from Medicare and Medicaid could offset new government spending for the plan, others, such as Senator Daniel Patrick Moynihan (D-NY), were dubious.

Even if the administration were right, about 120 million people would wind up paying more for health insurance coverage in just the first year. "If 40 percent of insured Americans are going to pay more, we're going to have to persuade some of those that they're going to get more and others that, on balance, it's their civic duty," noted Moynihan. "We're not always very good at that."

Proposed limits on premiums and requirements for universal coverage worried insurance companies, which stood to lose profits. To control costs, they would have to limit payments to health care providers and drug companies.

Right-to-life groups objected that the plan could pay for abortions. Health security cards and a central database presented worries about confidentiality and identity theft. Distrust of the government was another issue. "Can you imagine relying on a bureaucracy like the IRS to decide your health care needs?" asked Craig Weil, a Georgia physician.

The specter of rationing raised the biggest worries. Critics claimed that a national health care budget would inevitably lead to limits on the distribution of health care resources. Some people feared that patients would routinely get inadequate care or face long waits for treatment.

The Health Insurance Association of America fueled the public's fears with a $20 million media campaign. "But

National Health Care

what if there's not enough money?" asked one of the ads. The ads' fictional characters, Harry and Louise, liked their present plan just fine. They did not want the government to force them to change.

Republican politicians opposed the Clinton plan because of the burdens it would put on businesses. Also, they viewed defeating the Clinton plan as a way for their party to gain control of Congress.

The opposition succeeded in its aims. Fifty-nine percent of Americans had supported Clinton's plan when the president announced it in September 1993. Nine months later, only 33 percent thought the health care reform plan would be good for the country.

The plan's complexity was part of the problem. At 1,342 pages, it was too long for most people to read and understand. The task force had also failed to develop support among health care providers, employers, and other stakeholders before presenting its plan to the public.

When opponents attacked Clinton's plan, people were ready to listen. After various committee hearings, the plan died in Congress.

4
Healthy Competition?

Supporters of market-based reform believe the health care system will work better with less government intervention, rather than more. They promote the concept of a free market with competition among buyers and sellers of health care products.

This section looks at the health care market more closely and considers some market-based reforms. The following section will explore ideas for universal health programs with greater government involvement.

An Imperfect Market

Generally speaking, the United States' economy is a capitalist system. Under capitalist theory, as outlined by economist Adam Smith (1723–1790), if everyone acts in his or her economic self-interest, an efficient allocation of resources should result. Of course, the real world is far from ideal.

Buyers and sellers do not always behave the way eco-

National Health Care

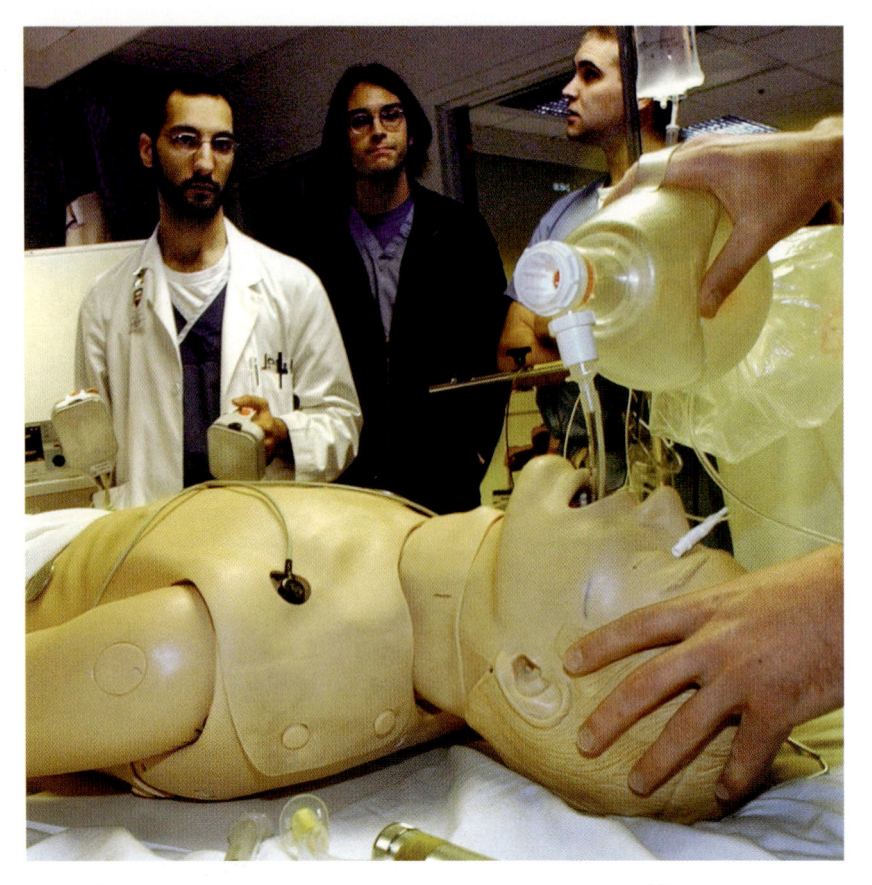

It costs a lot to train people to become doctors. Here, medical students practice their craft on a dummy in a medical simulation center.

nomic theory predicts. The classic capitalist model of economics assumes that supply and demand are elastic. In other words, sellers and buyers should respond to price changes by changing production or purchasing behavior. In the health care field, however, resources cannot shift quickly.

Many health care jobs require significant training and

education. In one sense, such requirements act as a barrier to entry into the field. Only individuals with the time, talent, and resources to invest in the field will undergo training. Afterward, those individuals expect significant compensation. Indeed, medical schools have generally limited their class sizes in order to prevent an oversupply of doctors.

With so much invested, medical professionals may not shift easily from one field to another. Nor are they likely to want to drop their "prices" far below certain levels.

Likewise, the number of health care facilities does not change quickly in response to consumer demand. Hospitals, clinics, and other facilities require substantial capital investments and have high operating costs. It is also expensive to buy and maintain the latest medical equipment for testing, surgery, and other procedures.

Demand is somewhat inelastic on the consumer side of the health care industry as well. When insurance does not cover services, people may put off regular physicals or skip doctor visits for relatively minor illnesses. Women, in particular, are likely to forgo routine but important health care procedures when price is an issue.

People who are extremely sick or badly injured, however, cannot just decide to do without medical attention. In other words, patients are sensitive to price concerns up to a point. Past that point, they "buy" medical services anyway.

Ironically, when people delay medical care because of costs, they often incur greater expenses down the road. By the time they do seek care, complications have often set in. Treating a disease or injury that has been neglected tends to be more difficult and expensive.

In fact, such patients typically wind up in hospital emergency rooms. In part this happens because the patients' conditions worsen to the point that they require

National Health Care

immediate attention. As a separate matter, the emergency room may be the only place such patients feel they can go. Regular clinics or doctor's offices do not have to treat non-emergency cases if patients cannot pay or lack insurance. However, many hospitals must provide emergency care without regard to ability to pay, as a condition for non-profit status for tax purposes. Ironically, hospital emergency room costs are generally much higher than those charged for regular doctor's office visits.

People who have health insurance do not respond according to the standard competitive model, either. Once any deductible has been spent, each additional use of health care services costs them only the copay amounts. Insurance does its job by insulating policyholders from the full burden of health care expenses.

However, that same feature blunts patients' sensitivity to price. People become more likely to use health services they might have done without if they had to pay the full cost out-of-pocket. Or they may reason that greater use of medical services is the best way to get their money's worth from the policy. Sue Blevins at the Cato Institute, a free-market advocacy group, uses the analogy of a group splitting a restaurant bill. For example, a nondrinker might order a dessert he might not otherwise have "to get his money's worth" when the rest of the group orders wine.

Insured patients do feel some effects of higher medical costs when they pay their share of health care premiums. When they get insurance through work, however, the employer's share cushions them from the full effects of premium price increases. Of course, workers may miss out on pay increases when employers' expenses for benefits go up. However, such effects are not readily apparent to many employees.

Also, workers generally have a limited choice of health plans, since most take what their employer offers. Employers generally want to choose a decent plan because good

Healthy Competition?

benefits attract qualified employees. However, companies are in business to make money. The plans that best help employers control costs are not necessarily the ones that workers would choose for themselves.

When employers fund their own plans under ERISA, workers' and employers' interests can diverge even more. The employer still wants to save on funding its plan. Moreover, the employer is now in the position of an insurance company. Just as insurers make more money when they pay out fewer claims, a business that funds its own plan fares better financially if the plan pays out fewer claims.

Insurance companies are probably the most sensitive to health care costs because they pay the bulk of patients' covered expenses. Since managed care became common, insurance companies have played a greater role in deciding which services patients would be able to buy. Again, though, insurers' interests differ from those of their policyholders.

Insurance relieves covered patients of the burden of huge costs for illness or injuries. However, insurance companies do not want to lose bets about whether covered patients will stay healthy. Rather, their aim is to pool risks and to collect enough to pay out expenses, with a profit left over. Usually insurers do that job well enough to stay in business.

Of course, the less an insurer pays out over the course of a year, the higher its profits will be. In any questionable case, then, insurers have an incentive to deny payment or coverage. As reports of insurance coverage disputes show, companies' decisions are often at odds with the choices of patients and their doctors.

In short, the health care market is nowhere near the ideal competitive market that economic theorists talk about. Yet it is still a market. Health care providers compete with each other to some extent. Insurance companies compete among themselves. Employers compete to attract qualified workers. And consumers make some choices about what health care services to buy.

Nevertheless, the imperfections and variations are significant. They affect the way the health care industry works. They also influence the extent to which market-based proposals can help cure America's health care system.

Health Savings Accounts

Health savings accounts (HSAs) came into existence in 2003. Although they expanded on an earlier pilot program for older people, HSAs are available to people of all ages.

Basically, HSAs combine one type of private insurance with a tax-preferred savings account just for health care spending. People get the HSA insurance policy through their employers or on their own. The insurance policy covers major medical expenses. However, it has a high deductible. As enacted, HSAs required deductible amounts between $1,050 and $5,250 for individuals, and between $2,100 and $10,500 for families. In other words, the policy will not pay anything until patients have spent the deductible amount for covered expenses.

Because of the high deductibles, HSA policies cost less than those with more comprehensive coverage. Employers save on overall insurance costs. Employees pay less for their share of the premium. More people can thus afford health insurance, at least for major expenses.

In 2004, for example, Mercury Office Supply in Minnesota would have had to pay $36,000 for its previous health insurance program for fourteen workers. Because the company became one of the first to offer HSAs, however, its health insurance costs for that year were just $24,000.

Healthy Competition?

Beyond this, HSAs offer a tax benefit that regular insurance does not. To pay for expenses under the deductible part of their plans, consumers deposit money into a special savings account. They do not pay tax on money in the account. Earnings on that money are also tax-free.

As long as the money from the account goes for a qualified health care expense, the decision to spend it is entirely up to the patient. Patients can use the accounts when they get sick or hurt. They can also use them to pay for regular checkups or general preventive care. Preventive care includes various measures for staying healthy and reducing the chance of illnesses.

If someone does not spend all the money in one year, it stays in the account earning interest. Individuals can spend the funds for health care in later years. They do not lose the money, the way they would if they had spent it for premiums on a traditional insurance policy.

President George W. Bush touted HSAs as a major move forward. The program could let more people get health insurance. At the same time, it would make patients more sensitive to the true costs of various health care services. That sensitivity could pressure the health care industry to control costs. As Bush said in a speech at the National Institutes of Health:

> **[H]ealth savings accounts all aim at empowering people to make decisions for themselves, owning their own health care plan, and at the same time, bringing some demand control into the cost of health care.**

At the same talk, the president urged loosening insurance restrictions, so that associations of small businesses could pool risks across state boundaries.

"HSAs put individuals in charge of their health care

National Health Care

TREASURY SECRETARY JOHN SNOW APPEARS AT A 2006 NEWS CONFERENCE PROMOTING HEALTH SAVINGS ACCOUNTS. HSAS COMBINE A HIGH-DEDUCTIBLE INSURANCE POLICY WITH A TAX-FREE SAVINGS ACCOUNT THAT CAN ONLY BE USED FOR MEDICAL PURPOSES.

purchasing decisions," Secretary of the Treasury John Snow told Congress. In his view, HSAs offer flexibility that traditional workplace health insurance does not. A person who leaves a job can take any health savings account along, just as people keep their individual retirement accounts. Self-employed individuals can participate also.

By 2007, nearly 5 million Americans had HSAs. Approximately one-quarter of them had previously been uninsured. "In other words," President Bush said, "health

Healthy Competition?

savings accounts enable someone who is uninsured to realize the benefits of private insurance, and in an affordable way."

The Heritage Foundation, a group that promotes free enterprise, limited government, and individual freedom, believes that HSAs are a positive step. Consumers get more control over health care spending. They also have ownership of their health savings accounts. However, says spokesperson Greg D'Angelo, HSAs are not a "silver bullet" for America's health care system. "They won't address everything."

Other groups, such as the advocacy group Families USA and the Century Foundation research organization, have more serious problems with HSAs. One issue is the high deductible. People who cannot afford standard insurance plans might welcome the lower HSA policy premium to cover major medical costs. However, many of them could face substantial hardship paying for non-covered deductible amounts.

High-deductible plans could also lead to less healthy choices. That could make America's health care costs higher, noted Ron Pollack at Families USA:

> **For American families on tight budgets, the President's proposal will make the health affordability crisis much worse. High-deductible insurance policies will force families to delay needed care, which will drive up costs in the long run as easy-to-treat conditions become expensive illnesses.**

Critics warn that HSAs might even make the problem of affordable health insurance worse. If enough healthy and well-to-do individuals decide that they would be better off with HSAs, their exit from traditional insurance programs would alter the relative risks faced by those who

Who Wins with Health Savings Accounts?

In 2006 the General Accounting Office (GAO) reported to Congress about the public's early experiences with HSAs. In general, the plans were most popular with healthy consumers who did not have huge ongoing medical expenses. The plans also appealed to well-to-do consumers who could afford the plans' average deductibles of $1,901 for a single person and $4,070 for families. In 2004 the average adjusted gross income for HSA owners was $133,000, more than twice the $51,000 average for the general population under age sixty-five. More than half the people with HSA accounts earned $75,000 or more.

Most HSA account holders surveyed in the study felt satisfied with the plans. Some of them comparison-shopped for medicines, although few did so for doctors, clinics, or hospitals.

Account holders did not uniformly recommend HSAs to others, though. They especially would not advise them for people with chronic conditions who need regular medication. Participants also were wary about recommending the plans to people with children or those who would struggle with the high deductible.

Adjusted Gross Income of Tax Filers Reporting HSA Contributions and All Tax Filers, 2004

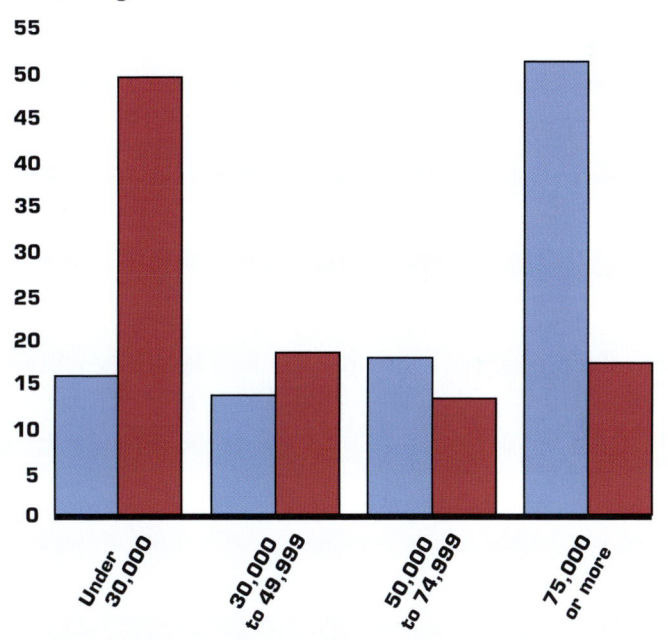

Percentage of tax filers

Adjusted gross income (in dollars)

- Tax filers reporting HSA contribution
- All tax filers

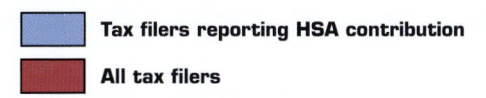

Source: General Accounting Office, 2006.

stay. Older and sicker people would most likely remain in the regular programs. Their claims as a group would rise, and so would their premiums. If more people kept leaving, a so-called death spiral might drive claims and premiums high enough to put an insurer out of business.

Ultimately, the debate comes down to one of perspective. Critics of HSAs say that society does better when health insurance covers a broader pool of individuals. HSAs' advocates say that the pooling of risks is best for unforeseen events. For routine health care, these advocates prefer to let individuals make their own spending choices.

Revise the Tax Laws

Changing the tax laws could make it easier for people to purchase policies on their own and might reduce the dominance of job-based health insurance. Such changes could help the health care market perform better as well.

In theory, each dollar an employer spends on health insurance is a dollar of forgone wages. If employers were not paying for workers' health insurance, they could offer higher salaries. Indeed, while the value of health benefits increased in private industry from 1970 to 1991, average take-home pay at the end of the period was about $200 lower.

However, workers do not pay tax on the amount an employer contributes toward their health insurance. If the employer paid that money to the workers first, the employees would be using after-tax dollars to buy their own insurance. The amount of coverage they could purchase would be less.

Because of the tax benefit, workers under the current system sometimes sign up for more insurance than they need or would otherwise buy with after-tax dollars. In the United States, people pay income taxes based on gradu-

Healthy Competition?

ated rates. In other words, the marginal tax rate increases as people's taxable income rises. (The "marginal rate" is the rate that applies to any additional dollars that someone earns. Thus, one rate applies to income up to a certain level, a higher rate applies to dollars earned above that amount and up to another level, and so on.)

The tax benefits of workplace-based insurance are thus greater for people in higher tax brackets. As a result, some top earners could come out ahead by choosing another $100 worth of insurance, even if their expenses without the extra coverage would be only $75.

In theory, the government could just eliminate Section 106 of the Internal Revenue Code. That is the provision that lets people exclude the value of workplace health insurance from gross income. Without that exclusion, government revenues might go up by $125 billion to $200 billion.

However, it seems unlikely that the government would make such a major change without further reforms. Without the tax benefit, people who already have trouble paying their share of premiums for workplace coverage would have even fewer after-tax dollars to pay for health insurance and other budget items.

Also, employers would have less incentive to offer workplace coverage without any tax exclusion. The present health insurance market is geared toward the existing environment, with better rates for larger groups. Nevertheless, the inequality in the present tax code remains a concern.

"Changing the tax code is a vital and necessary step to making health care affordable for more Americans," President Bush said in his 2007 State of the Union address. Toward that end, Bush proposed a standard tax deduction for health insurance, equal to $15,000 for families and $7,500 for individuals. "[F]or the millions of . . .

National Health Care

Americans who have no health insurance at all, this deduction would help put a basic private health insurance plan within their reach."

Bush estimated the tax savings at $4,500 for a four-person family earning $60,000 per year. A family with no health coverage could use that money to offset the cost of insurance. People with workplace health insurance would save on taxes, too.

To offset revenue losses, Bush proposed taxing workplace health care benefits worth more than $15,000. Below that value, premiums paid by an employer would still be tax-free. Thus, people with workplace health care coverage would still fare better.

Families USA argued that the Bush proposal fell far short of giving real relief to uninsured people with low or moderate incomes. "It's like throwing a 10-foot rope to someone in a 40-foot hole," says spokesperson Ron Pollack.

Deductions work by reducing taxable income. Thus, the higher someone's marginal tax rate is, the greater value a deduction has. As of 2007, people earning less than $31,850 had a marginal income tax rate of 15 percent. At most, Bush's proposal would save them only $1,125 in taxes. Meanwhile, to get the deduction, uninsured people would have to buy health insurance, plus pay any related deductibles and copayments. "[T]herefore the new tax deduction will provide precious little relief," says Pollack.

Families USA believes that a tax credit would be fairer than a tax deduction. Even though the Heritage Foundation called Bush's proposal a "bold step forward," it too felt that a tax credit would be "even better." The American Medical Association has also come out in favor of a system of tax credits for health insurance.

A tax credit is a dollar-for-dollar offset against a person's total tax bill. Generally, tax credits are subtracted from the total amount owed in taxes. The child tax credit provides an example. As of 2007, taxpayers could subtract $1,000 from their final tax bill for each qualifying child in their household. However, the tax credit's value could not exceed the taxpayer's total tax liability.

The Cato Institute suggests capping the total amount of credit available. That way, people would not have an incentive to spend more on health care just to lower their taxes. The system would not favor health care spending over spending for other goods and services.

Note that tax credits can also be structured to give money back to people. One example is the earned income credit, which helps qualified low-income people who work and have dependent children. People who qualify subtract the credit from their low or zero-amount tax bills. The government then pays the individuals the amount it "owes." In this way, the program transfers money from the government to private citizens.

In theory, the same concept could be used to help people purchase health insurance. Whether different interest groups favor a refundable tax credit depends on several factors. For example, do they want the government to subsidize people buying private health insurance? If so, do they want to use the tax system or another mechanism for that purpose?

Creating a Nationwide Health Insurance Market

One way to change the health care system would be to set up a nationwide insurance market. Presently, individual states regulate the sale of health insurance, except for employers' self-funded plans. In general, rates charged for premiums depend on the experience and cost levels within an individual state. National insurance companies exist, but they tailor plans to the requirements of different states and sell them only within those states. Individuals buying insurance outside the workplace must choose from plans offered in their states.

Groups that favor less government regulation, like the Heritage Foundation and the National Center for Policy Analysis, favor interstate sales of health insurance. A nationwide market could create larger risk pools. It would also increase competition among insurers. Individuals and families could benefit from these effects through more affordable health insurance premiums.

Senator Jim DeMint (R-SC) and Representative John Shadegg (R-AZ) introduced bills to allow such interstate sales in 2005. Under their proposal, a program that met any one state's requirements could be sold in any other state. The plan did not pass.

Families USA believed that the proposed Health Care Choice Act would have been a move "in the wrong direction." Presumably, a plan would only have to meet the least restrictive regulations of any state. Those plans would provide the fewest protections for consumers, as well as less coverage. Since less protective plans attract relatively healthy consumers, people who are older or sicker would remain in higher-priced plans. A death spiral of sicker patients and higher premiums could put the companies offering more comprehensive plans out of business. Meanwhile, many consumers would be underinsured.

The Democratic staff for the House Committee on Energy and Commerce also criticized the proposal's lack of consumer protections. At the time, for example, forty-six states required health insurance plans to cover diabetes. Under the proposed bill, insurers could avoid covering the disease simply by going through one of the jurisdictions that did not mandate such coverage. Similarly, companies could avoid the requirements of many states for health plans to cover maternity care, mental illness, asthma, cancer, or other conditions.

At present, states also set requirements for insurance companies' financial stability. They require insurers to have sufficient assets at hand to pay claims without delay. Under the proposed bills, however, companies that met the lowest standards could have sold insurance in all fifty states. Potentially, insurers might have been unable to pay patient claims in a timely manner.

Other criticisms focus on potential regulatory nightmares. Presently, consumers can complain about problems to their state insurance regulators. With a nationwide market, consumers could have trouble determining where to bring complaints. State regulatory agencies might also have problems handling disputes across the nation.

Statewide Health Insurance Exchanges

If a nationwide insurance market is not feasible, perhaps the state markets could function more competitively. From this standpoint, the Heritage Foundation has promoted the concept of statewide health insurance exchanges. Several state health care initiatives have adopted or used versions of the idea.

A health insurance exchange would basically be a central market for buying coverage. An independent body set up by the government would provide a clearinghouse with information on available policies. That independent body would also keep records and collect premiums.

One can compare a health insurance exchange to a farmers' market that offers products from many suppliers. Some suppliers compete with each other directly, as when multiple stalls sell zucchini or mushrooms. Other suppliers offer similar but different products, such as the beef and pork counters. Yet other suppliers, such as the cheese stand and the fresh fish booth, offer vastly different products. Buyers wander through the market, decide what they want, and make deals with individual sellers.

Similarly, a stock exchange is a central place where people can make investments. In the United States, the Securities and Exchange Commission has rules to prevent fraud. Subject to those rules, companies can sell a wide variety of stocks, bonds, commodities, and other financial interests. Sellers pay whatever the market price is at the time of the transaction.

The Massachusetts Connector presently works as an exchange to offer health insurance to individuals and small businesses. However, the Heritage Foundation would prefer that any exchange also be open to all businesses on a voluntary basis. An employer could designate the exchange as its health plan for federal tax purposes and state how much it would pay in premiums.

Employees would then shop on the exchange to pick their policies. They could pay any difference between the premium and the employer's contribution by having the employer deduct that amount from their wages. Significantly, workers who left their job could keep the same health insurance policy. In other words, consumers would own their policies, not employers.

Under the Heritage Foundation's proposal, a health insurance exchange would have a very low level of regulatory oversight. Basically, companies could offer any type of insurance, from bare-bones policies with high deductibles to programs offering comprehensive coverage. Supporters say that would lead to the most competition in a free market.

Several benefits would theoretically flow from the proposed health insurance exchange. The present system splits the insurance market into large groups, small groups, and

Healthy Competition?

individuals. With a unified exchange, costs for many people could go down. That would make health insurance more affordable, supporters say.

Presently, many people become uninsured for several months when they change employment. With an exchange, people could keep their health insurance coverage when moving from job to job or when they are between jobs. An exchange would also weaken the strong link between the workplace and health care coverage. People would find it easier to obtain health care coverage on their own, say supporters.

Businesses would like the proposal's emphasis on voluntary participation. Supporters say that consumers would have more choices and could select plans based on their personal situations.

Selections could also reflect consumers' personal beliefs. For example, someone who opposes abortion could pick a plan that did not cover that procedure. Someone who does not smoke might prefer not to share the health care costs of people who do.

Instead of having a separate Medicaid system, the Heritage Foundation would have the exchange provide insurance premium support for low-income families. Families could then purchase whatever health insurance best fit their needs. Likewise, instead of a separate public program for children's insurance, a state could provide funds equal to the cost of private coverage for the children. Parents could then purchase policies just for their children. Or they could apply the money to a policy for the whole family. That option might be more convenient and less confusing for many people.

Critics like the Center on Budget and Policy Priorities (CBPP) say an exchange should not substitute for present aid, such as Medicaid or children's health insurance programs. The research organization focuses on public

National Health Care

policies that affect low- and moderate-income people. They worry that states might reduce funding for poor people and children. Or families might choose policies without comprehensive coverage. CBPP also believes that any exchange should set minimum standards.

Heath insurance products offered through the Massachusetts Connector must meet various standards for coverage. Other jurisdictions, including Maryland and the District of Columbia, have also considered state health insurance exchanges. However, such state programs and proposals stop short of the complete free market advocated by the Heritage Foundation and similar groups.

5
Universal Health Care: A Major Medical Makeover

Champions of universal health care say Americans cannot afford to let the market take care of the system's problems. The market has not stopped the upward spiral of health care costs and insurance premiums. Nor does it protect the country's millions of uninsured and underinsured people.

Instead, universal health supporters say the system needs a major overhaul. They demand broader government involvement and mandatory participation.

Various political candidates have come out in favor of universal health care. The concept also has support from groups like AARP, the Alzheimer's Association, the American Heart Association, the American Diabetes Association, and the American Cancer Society Cancer Action Network.

Advocates vary on whether they want a single-payer system run by the government or a mix of public and private options. Nevertheless, they note, every other developed country provides some form of national health care for all its citizens. In 2004 the Institute of Medicine of the

National Health Care

THESE CALIFORNIA NURSES JOIN HUNDREDS OF OTHERS IN A 2007 RALLY CALLING FOR A SINGLE-PAYER, UNIVERSAL HEALTH CARE SYSTEM.

National Academy of Sciences called upon political leaders in the United States to provide universal health coverage for everyone by 2010. Debate on the issue is under way.

A Matter of Values

Supporters of universal health care share a general view that the government should make sure everyone gets some basic level of health care. Admittedly, the Constitution

Universal Health Care: A Major Medical Makeover

contains no express right to health care. Some federal programs, such as Medicare and Medicaid, provide treatment for groups of people. The Emergency Medical Treatment and Active Labor Act of 1986 provides access to emergency treatment regardless of ability to pay. However, emergency treatment covers limited situations. No federal law yet requires basic health care for all Americans.

Nevertheless, some universal health care advocates say, such care should be considered a basic right. As Thomas C. Kelly, a Roman Catholic bishop in Kentucky put it,

Access to basic health care is a fundamental human right, necessary for the development and maintenance of life and for the ability of human beings to realize the fullness of their dignity.

Access to health care is indeed a matter of life and death. According to the Institute of Medicine, lack of health insurance causes approximately 18,000 unnecessary deaths each year. Risa Lavizzo-Mourey, president and CEO of the Robert Wood Johnson Foundation, compared that loss to having the September 11 deaths "recur six times over every year, year after year."

Some supporters of universal health care compare it with the right to a public education. The rationale is that everyone needs a basic education to function in our society. Whether children receive that education should not depend on how rich their families are or whether the parents make schooling a priority. Thus, while parents can choose private alternatives, every state offers a basic public education for all children. Moreover, students with special needs and disabilities have a federally guaranteed right to a free public education, based on individualized plans.

Similarly, supporters say, the ability to get necessary

National Health Care

medical care should not depend on the ability to afford insurance. People do not choose to be born into families that cannot afford health care. Even if someone has health insurance today, the present system offers no guarantee that it will be available or affordable in the future. If one person loses health insurance, a whole family may be at risk.

Free public education protects society from some of the adverse consequences of an uneducated population. Those societal costs include higher unemployment, lost productivity, increases in crime and poverty, and so forth. When people cannot afford health care, their illnesses impose costs on society, too.

Indeed, when people without health insurance finally receive emergency care, their conditions have often become more serious, thus requiring more expensive measures. Ultimately, the result is higher charges and higher insurance premiums for other individuals. Taxpayers also bear a portion of the costs through public aid programs. Meanwhile, society loses the benefits of its citizens' productivity.

Beyond this, good or poor health is often a matter of chance. Yes, personal choices have a huge impact on health. For example, smoking greatly increases the risk of illness and premature death. Regular exercise and a healthy diet improve the chances for good health. However, serious disease can and does strike people even when they make wise choices.

Chance also plays a role in the ability to pay for health care. "No one is certain, even if they have really good health insurance, that the vicissitudes [unexpected changes] of life won't hit them," notes Roger Hickey, co-director of the Campaign for America's Future. "If you lose your employment, especially, all that security goes away."

Socioeconomic factors play a big part too. The least

Universal Health Care: A Major Medical Makeover

healthy groups in the United States are also those with the lowest incomes and education levels. Individual choices make some difference, but most people who are poor do not choose that status.

Racial differences also exist, reports the Centers for Disease Control and Prevention (CDC). Compared to Caucasians, age-adjusted death rates for African Americans are about 25 percent higher for cancer and more than 100 percent higher for diabetes. Infant mortality rates for black babies are 130 percent greater than those for whites. Advocates for change deplore such differences in health outcomes.

In short, our individual choices cannot fully determine whether we are sick or well or whether we can afford health care. Health care is not an "optional luxury," says Yale political science professor Jacob Hacker. Rather, our society should provide basic health protection to everyone.

Altruism is not the only reason that supporters favor universal health care. American businesses pay roughly $500 billion in health care costs every year. "This cost has crowded out wage increases, business investments, and hurt our global competitiveness," notes former Senator Tom Daschle.

Universal health care supporters believe that reform can reduce the country's current $2 trillion bill for health care, while cutting costs to businesses. Potential benefits would include higher wages and greater job security, along with reduced worries about health. More resources would also become available for other needs.

"Health care is a right, not a privilege," argued Representative Dennis Kucinich (D-OH) in 2007. His second bid for the Democratic presidential nomination was almost certain to fail. Yet polls showed that nearly two-thirds of Americans thought that the government should guarantee health insurance for everyone.

"It isn't about *them*," argues *New Republic* editor

National Health Care

Jonathan Cohn. "It's about *us*." He and other universal health care supporters may disagree on details. Yet they all believe that our democracy should guarantee basic health protection for everyone.

Paying with Private and Public Resources

America's health care system already depends upon a combination of public and private payers. On the private side, payments come from insurance programs or directly from patients. On the public side, Medicare covers elderly people, while Medicaid pays the bills for low-income patients. In addition, many health care providers also perform a significant amount of services without pay. They either do without the money or build the written-off or donated amounts into other charges as part of the cost of doing business.

Some supporters say that it makes sense to design a universal health care system that combines public and private resources. However, they caution, proposals should not be so complex that they scare people off. Complexity made the Clinton health security proposal a harder sell in 1994. It also confounded the public when presidential candidate John Kerry proposed a federal reinsurance program in 2004. (Reinsurance is a way for insurers to pass off some of their risks by buying insurance from other companies.)

One proposal for a simpler plan comes from Yale political science professor Jacob Hacker, the Economic Policy Institute, and the Campaign for America's Future. Under a Medicare-plus plan, employers would have two choices. One choice would be to provide all employees with health care coverage that meets specific standards set by the government.

Alternatively, employers would pay a percentage of

Universal Health Care: A Major Medical Makeover

their payroll to a government-run Medicare-type insurance program. The program would offer low-cost comprehensive insurance to people who did not have health coverage through an employer. Self-employed individuals could participate also. People presently covered by Medicare and poor people would not have to pay for the government program.

"The goal, of course, of our approach is to get as large a group of people into a public plan as possible," notes Roger Hickey, "but without forcing people to join it if they don't want to." Anyone who still had insurance through the workplace would be offered a program at least as comprehensive as the public one.

Using Medicare as the foundation for the public part of the program has several advantages, supporters say. Medicare has functioned for more than forty years. The public generally understands the concept. Most important, despite bureaucratic hassles, gaps in coverage, and other issues, senior citizens generally like Medicare. As former Medicare administrator Tom Scully says, "Seniors love it."

Another proposal from the Center for American Progress (CAP) would also draw on public and private resources. An expanded Medicaid program would provide more low-income Americans with basic health care. Other Americans would choose private health coverage from a new group insurance pool.

The group pool would resemble the system presently used by Congress and federal employees. People would review different insurance plans each year and choose whatever made the most sense for them. Unlike the Heritage Foundation's proposal, plans would have to provide a minimum level of coverage, as determined by the government. CAP believes its proposal would make sure not only that all Americans have insurance, but also that such insurance is adequate.

CAP's proposal would use refundable tax credits to

prevent health care costs from exceeding a fixed percentage of income. That level would depend on the results of studies on affordability, but might be in the range of 5 to 7.5 percent.

"If you have a refundable tax credit, that is money you would receive regardless of whether you have an income tax liability," notes Karen Davenport at CAP. Thus, if the credit exceeded someone's tax liability, the government would pay the difference.

Money for government spending under CAP's plan would come from a new value-added tax, or VAT. With a VAT, each person along the commerce chain, from production to final sale, collects a tax based on the amount received for a good or service and the amount paid to suppliers. Exceptions for items like food and clothing could keep the tax from overburdening middle- and lower-income families.

By keeping parts of the present system, public-private health care plans would involve less drastic change. People who are reasonably happy with their current situation would feel less threatened. At the same time, mandates for coverage would expand insurance coverage dramatically.

Nonetheless, universal health plans will face opposition. Critics will complain about costs to businesses, limits on choices, regulatory burdens, and other perceived disadvantages. Expansion of government funding for health care will be a huge sticking point, as well.

One Payer, One System

In some countries, the government pays directly for all citizens' health care. Great Britain, Canada, and France are a few examples. These governments cover a broad range of services, and patients need not carry insurance to qualify for basic care.

Some health reform advocates want a single-payer sys-

Universal Health Care: A Major Medical Makeover

tem in the United States. Supporters include the consumer advocacy group Public Citizen, various labor organizations, and Physicians for a National Health Program. The 2007 Michael Moore documentary, *Sicko*, also promoted a single-payer system.

Details of proposed single-payer programs vary. One possibility is a "Medicare for All" program like that proposed by Representatives John Conyers (D-MI) and Dennis Kucinich (D-OH) in 2003. The government would become the single payer for all medically necessary services. Coverage would include inpatient and outpatient care, emergency care, prescription medicines, long-term care, mental health and substance abuse treatment, eye care, and dental services. Patients would not have to pay any deductibles or make any copayments for covered services.

Delivery of medical services would take place through private physicians and nonprofit facilities. The federal program would reset doctors' reimbursement rates every year. It would also determine total payments for health care providers' operating expenses. The national office would negotiate prices for prescription drugs with manufacturers. Existing Medicare offices would administer payments within their respective regions.

To pay for the program, the sponsors proposed a payroll tax of 3.3 percent on all employers. The country's top 5 percent of income earners would pay an extra 5 percent health tax as well. As of 2004, that group included most households earning $150,000 or more. Taxes on stock and bond transfers, repeals of prior tax cuts, and changes in corporate tax provisions would help make up the difference between the proposed program and current federal and state funding for government health programs.

The proposed single-payer program would prohibit any private health insurance plans that duplicated its coverage. For-profit health care facilities would also have to

National Health Care

convert to nonprofit status. Conversion to the all-public, nonprofit program would take place over fifteen years.

Supporters say that a single-payer plan would be simplest and most efficient. Under the present system, administrative expenses consume approximately 30 percent of total health costs. Health care providers must fill out dozens of different forms to get paid. Insurance company practices often produce delays of several months between performance of services and collection of payment. Meanwhile, facilities send out multiple bills.

With a single-payer system, there would be only one claims form, and all health care providers would have to use it. This system would consolidate the resources that multiple private insurers now spend to process claims. It would also eliminate most current disputes about exclusions from coverage, questions about who pays if more than one policy might apply, and other issues.

To illustrate potential savings, a 2003 study noted that Canada's health administration costs per capita were slightly more than $300 per person. The United States spent over $1,050 per person, more than three times as much.

With a single-payer system, everyone would get coverage, regardless of medical history, age, or other factors. Workers would no longer have to worry about losing an employer's health benefits. The system would cut the link between the workplace and health insurance. People would have coverage even if they changed jobs, lost jobs, or never worked.

In contrast to a private, profit-driven system, supporters of a single-payer health care system say it would be publicly accountable. Although ways to ensure accountability vary, the country's new health czars would answer to the president. They would also have to report to Congress as part of annual budget proceedings and other legislative

Universal Health Care: A Major Medical Makeover

inquiries. Program records would be open to the public, subject to limits in the Freedom of Information Act or other laws.

People might not agree with all of the program's actions and policies. However, its leaders would make decisions in an atmosphere of openness. Supporters of universal health care say that would be fairer than the present system.

A single-payer program would involve the most change from the current system. For one thing, the system would replace the present private insurance industry. As a result, hundreds of thousands of people would have to find new jobs. Insurance company shareholders would also lose all or most of the value of their investments. Meanwhile, any new government health agency would lack the years of experience that today's insurers have. Even if it hired some experienced people, the agency would be starting from scratch.

Meanwhile, citizens and employers would have no choice but to use the new agency. As California Governor Arnold Schwarzenegger argued when he vetoed a single-payer health care bill for that state in 2006:

Socialized medicine is not the solution to our state's health care problems. This bill would require an extraordinary redirection of public and private funding by creating a vast new bureaucracy to take over health insurance and medical care for Californians—a serious and expensive mistake.

Universal health care would not necessarily lead to equal health care, either. OECD researchers found that even in countries that have a single-payer system, richer patients still saw doctors, including specialists, more frequently than poorer people. One reason is probably that

| National Health Care |

CALIFORNIA GOVERNOR ARNOLD SCHWARZENEGGER VISITS AN EMERGENCY ROOM PATIENT AT A SAN DIEGO HOSPITAL IN 2007. SCHWARZENEGGER'S PROPOSED HEALTH PLAN CALLED FOR MOST EMPLOYERS TO PROVIDE HEALTH INSURANCE OR TO PAY INTO A FUND THAT WOULD HELP PEOPLE BUY THEIR OWN POLICIES. INSURERS COULD NOT REFUSE COVERAGE ON THE GROUNDS OF AGE OR PREEXISTING CONDITIONS.

some patients in those countries also carry private insurance, either on their own or as a job benefit.

Almost surely, a single-payer system would lock health care providers into binding fee schedules to control costs. Doctors, administrators, and others in the health care industry would face cutbacks and would lose whatever freedom they have in setting fees and charges. Limits on income would make the industry less attractive to newcomers. In addition, businesses would lose a profit incentive to invest in research and development for new technological innovations.

Universal Health Care: A Major Medical Makeover

In short, argues AMA past president J. Edward Hill, a single-payer system would stifle innovation, discourage investment, and eliminate free choice and individual enterprise. In his view, that would be "simply, obviously wrong" and "simply, obviously unethical."

"They've done a good job of scaring people into thinking the federal government is bad," counters filmmaker Michael Moore. Yet no one argues that a government-run military is wrong. Nor do people object to government-run police and fire departments. For supporters of a single-payer system, government-run health insurance is the best choice, too.

The Bottom Line

Universal health care would be expensive. After all, its aim is to provide more health care for the millions of Americans who are presently uninsured and underinsured. On the other hand, greater access to expensive treatments means that health care costs would almost certainly rise.

Experience with the federal Medicare program supports such forecasts. In the first four years after the program took effect, hospital spending rose by 37 percent. Such increased costs were not necessarily bad. Older people were getting needed care and benefiting from new technologies.

However, argues Diana Ernst of the Pacific Research Institute, a conservative policy group, Medicare presently "devours the finances of working Americans." In her view, universal health coverage would drastically add to taxpayers' burdens.

By one estimate, health coverage for uninsured people could cost close to $170 billion a year. As of 2007, health care spending by or for that group already ran around $125 billion. Universal health coverage would bring those costs together and add another $45 billion. Other groups might also use more health services, especially underinsured people or those with high-deductible plans.

It is also unclear whether suggested sources of revenue would be enough to pay for universal health care. Both single-payer plans and private-public plans for universal coverage would rely on higher taxes. But universal health care supporters say their plans would also save money. Simplified paperwork could drastically cut administrative costs. The government could negotiate lower prices for services and medicines. More timely care could cut overall costs also.

Although universal coverage would cost more initially, supporters feel that over time it could trim the country's overall health care spending. Opponents of universal health care say that supporters are underestimating the costs and overstating possible savings. In reality, they argue, the costs are prohibitive. With current spending levels exceeding $2 trillion, however, supporters of universal coverage say that the United States is not getting its money's worth now.

Is Fear of Rationing Rational?

Opponents of universal health care argue that it will lead to rationing. Inevitably, any single-payer program will function under the auspices of a government agency. Even a public-private mix would have the government paying medical bills for a larger number of people. The program would have a limited amount of money to spend on care in any given year. As a result, its budget and spending decisions would affect the quality and quantity of medical services. Invariably, some medical services would not be performed.

Some critics of universal coverage point to Canada and Great Britain as examples of what can go wrong. While

Universal Health Care: A Major Medical Makeover

practicing medicine in Canada, one physician encountered a man who waited two years before getting into a pain clinic. When that doctor's own father suffered from a spinal condition, he had to wait six months for an MRI procedure.

In Great Britain, about 900,000 patients wait to get into hospitals at any given time. Reports from Sweden show waiting periods of more than a year for hip replacements, and nearly six months for heart surgery. For many people in the United States, such delays are unacceptable.

Because of delays, people in some countries with universal health care carry private health insurance, too. Often the insurance is a job benefit. Much as companies in the United States began providing health benefits when they could not increase salaries, some companies abroad are finding that health care is a popular job perk for upper-level employees. Sometimes the insurance covers extra services beyond the government program. But its biggest advantage is better access to basic care.

Formerly, Canada's system forbade private financing for services covered by its plan. Nonetheless, private clinics have sprung up around the country. In 2005 Canada's Supreme Court overturned the private health insurance ban in Quebec, citing evidence that patients were suffering on long waiting lists.

Supporters of universal health care reform do not deny the possibility that some rationing may occur. After all, no country has unlimited resources. People simply cannot get everything they want.

"Currently in the United States we ration enormously," observes Roger Hickey. "It's done on the basis of ability to pay."

In a capitalist economic system, competition deals with the problems of limited supply. Buyers who are willing and able to pay the most can purchase what they want.

National Health Care

Other buyers will be out of luck if the desired good or service is in short supply.

If unmet demands continue, other suppliers will enter the market. Additional supply lowers price somewhat, so that more buyers can satisfy their wants. If competition drives prices too low, however, suppliers will stop entering the market. In theory, the system eventually reaches equilibrium. In any marketplace, though, the wants of some people will never be met if they are unwilling or unable to pay the market price.

Speaking at a congressional hearing on behalf of CAP, former senator Daschle elaborated on the myth of rationing:

> **This ignores the fact that we ration now. Health care is delayed or denied to the uninsured and under-insured. Cancer can mean bankruptcy and asthma can consume college funds. Being older or sicker, or even having a family history, can make a person uninsurable—doomed to spend years worrying about the next illness's financial rather than health implications.**

Price is not the only way the present system rations health care. Lengthy waits on hold, annoying computerized phone systems, and insurance requirements make it difficult to schedule appointments. Even then, long delays are common in many hospitals, clinics, and doctors' offices. Patients often have shorter consultations and must return multiple times.

People may not think of these inconveniences as rationing. Yet they effectively limit people's health care services, even when insurance pays the bills. When one considers such types of rationing, America's present system compares less favorably to those of other countries. As Daschle explains:

Patient Experiences Abroad

Each time a patient seeks medical care, that person tests the effectiveness of one health care system or another. Personal experiences can highlight both the strengths and weaknesses of any universal care program.

For example, Ann H. likes the fact that the British national health system covers nearly everyone for a very reasonable cost. When her mother needed hip replacement surgery, the out-of-pocket cost was equivalent to about forty dollars. On the downside, however, Ann's mother had to wait a year for the operation. During that time, the older woman suffered frequent pain and discomfort.

Mike M. barely had to wait at all when he had a kidney stone attack while on vacation in Rome. As soon as a taxi dropped him and his wife at a hospital emergency room, a nurse brought him to an examination room. Less than ten minutes after that, a doctor saw him and ordered intravenous (IV) pain medication.

"They were very efficient at getting you to see a doctor quickly," notes Mike. Fortunately, the pain did not return after the IV drip, possibly because the stone had moved. Had Mike needed microsurgery or another procedure to remove or break up the obstruction, however, the Italian system would not have helped him. Instead, Mike would have had to wait until his return to the United States.

National Health Care

Thirty percent of sick Americans have access to same-day care, compared to 45 percent in the United Kingdom. Americans find it three times harder to get care at night and on weekends without going to emergency rooms compared to those in New Zealand. And we are more likely to have to wait to see a specialist than sick people in Germany. It's ironic that the U.S., compared to its competitor nations, offers fewer people less accessible care.

America's health care system also costs much more than other countries' programs do. Yet the United States still has its own form of rationing, with poorer results on measures of general health. Universal health care supporters say that arguments about rationing distract policy makers from the real need, which is for reform.

6
Prognosis for the Future

Ultimately, health care policy in the United States is not just about how people pay for medical services. It is about whether people can enjoy better health as well.

The Maze of Managed Care

Critics fear that necessary cost limits in universal health care programs will lead to rationing. To some extent, managed care programs already impose a form of rationing through their barriers and restrictions. Since the 1980s, managed care programs have tried to rein in health care costs. These efforts, in turn, affect the care patients get.

In general, managed care plans require extra steps before insurers will cover various procedures. Medical personnel may provide input on standards for approving various types of care. However, the staff person making the initial decision to approve or deny certain care is rarely a physician.

Many plans require advance approval for expensive or

National Health Care

complicated procedures. Basically, the plan imposes a gatekeeper between the patient and the health care provider. Some programs require a second opinion. Often a patient also needs a referral from a primary care physician to see a specialist. Extra approval from the insurer may be necessary, too.

Other plans review procedures after the fact. If the insurer disagrees with the health care provider's reasons for various services, it may deny payment.

Ideally, managed care programs would eliminate waste and inefficiency. They can discourage unnecessary and possibly risky medical procedures. They can help patients understand their options and make informed choices. In theory, then, managed care can be a win-win situation for both patients and insurers.

Consider the Back Pain Recognition Program set up by the National Committee for Quality Assurance (NCQA). The group's main mission is to improve the quality of health care. Thirty million Americans suffer from back pain, and treatment costs exceed $90 billion each year. Not all the NCQA's guidelines recommend the cheapest care. In most cases, however, acute back pain problems resolve themselves within six weeks. Until that time has passed, surgery, X rays, CT scans, and various other steps are generally premature. Absent certain conditions or symptoms, the better course is usually pain management with a return to physical activity after a short period of bed rest.

While NCQA focuses on quality, insurers will use the program to control costs. According to one study, insurers could save $205 annually for each back pain patient if health care providers follow the guidelines. "This program will encourage our policyholders' employees who suffer from back pain to seek providers who excel at treating their back pain, while reducing unnecessary treatment and

Prognosis for the Future

costs," notes David Deitz at Liberty Mutual Group. "In the case of back pain, good medicine and cost containment are on the same side of the equation."

Managed care programs also offer a means of reviewing the quality of patient care. One study looked back at nearly 18,000 elderly patients under managed care. The researchers found that 39 percent used at least one potentially inappropriate medication. Such information alerts physicians to the need for greater care in prescribing drugs. Ideally, managed care might provide a backup check on the appropriateness of medications before patients suffer ill health effects.

In practice, however, managed care has garnered significant criticisms. In one New York survey, health plan denials of care or coverage topped patients' lists of health care complaints. "New Yorkers continue to encounter numerous obstacles when accessing and utilizing health care services," said Eliot Spitzer, who served as the state's attorney general.

When an insurer denies care that a physician has recommended, the company basically overrules the doctor. Many physicians disapprove of such second-guessing by someone who usually has no firsthand knowledge about a patient's condition. In one study, nine out of ten physicians reported incidents in which insurers had prevented their patients from getting care that the doctors deemed necessary.

Sometimes patients suffer as a result. A California woman with breast cancer died after her HMO refused to cover a bone marrow transplant. A baby boy in Georgia had permanent disabilities after an HMO routed him to a distant hospital, instead of letting him get treatment closer to home.

Families of both patients recovered millions of dollars in damages. In other cases, patients have little legal re-

National Health Care

course. Most large employers and even some smaller ones offer health plans as part of benefits packages covered by ERISA. Rather than deal with the details themselves, employers often contract with insurance companies or HMOs to administer the health care plans.

In such cases, federal law preempts state law in disputes about health benefits. An unhappy employee might sue under ERISA to get back the cost of the health benefit or to force its payment. Yet the employee could not legally pursue other remedies under state tort laws. (A tort is a wrongful act or omission committed against a private person, for which the law provides a civil remedy.)

Thus, in *Aetna Health Inc. v. Davila*, the Supreme Court said that two patients could not recover damages under Texas medical malpractice law because their health plans were covered by ERISA. Although the patients' lawyers argued that insurers' decisions made their health worse, neither could recover damages to compensate for that or any other monies that state tort law might have let them collect.

Basically, *Davila* and similar cases viewed patients' claims as disputes over benefits, rather than medical decisions. The American Bar Association Standing Committee on Medical Professional Liability and other groups support changing the ERISA law to allow state remedies. So far, this has not happened.

Even if patients do not get sicker, many feel frustrated when insurers deny care that their physicians recommend. After paying their share of the premiums, they want the insurer to cover whatever treatments their doctors prescribe.

One solution might be to place the burden of proof on insurers who deny coverage. A 2007 proposal in Connecticut, for example, would make insurers show why a recommended test or procedure was not necessary before they could deny a claim on that ground. State attorney general Richard Blumenthal said the bill would "restore consumer

Prognosis for the Future

control over health care decisions." The Connecticut Association of Health Plans argued that the bill, if enacted, would raise premiums because plans would then have to cover almost anything. ERISA could also limit any state law's application.

Patients have felt particularly frustrated when plans put physicians in potential conflict-of-interest situations. In various cases, HMOs have paid doctors on the basis of capitation. In other words, the organization paid doctors a certain amount per patient per year, regardless of how many services any individual might need. Such a system shifts the financial risks for sicker patients away from the insurer to the physicians. The health care provider then has an incentive to provider fewer services.

Back in the 1990s, "gag clauses" caused major problems under managed care. Contract terms between insurers and doctors often limited physicians' ability to discuss all their patients' treatment options fully. The clauses also prevented physicians from criticizing the quality of coverage provided by a plan. Instead, they were supposed to steer each patient toward the cheapest option.

The AMA challenged gag clauses as unethical, and HMOs generally no longer use them. Nonetheless, that practice and others left many doctors and patients with a strong distrust for managed care insurers.

As a result, there is a trend toward more consumer-driven plans. As Karen Davenport of the Center for American Progress sees it, "A lot of the teeth of managed care have been blunted if not actually pulled." Although Congress has not yet passed a federal patient bill of rights, various states have enacted protections for patients. When offered a choice by their employers, consumers who feel strongly can also pick plans that allow greater leeway in choosing physicians. Such plans may cost more than other options, though.

Nevertheless, some restrictions remain. Some patients

continue to have problems getting insurers to pay for procedures their doctors recommend. Delays, red tape, and inflexibility add to problems, too. The profit motive acts as an incentive for insurance companies to deny or delay claims payment in any borderline case.

As a separate matter, if plans were to lift all restrictions, concerns about cost containment would grow. In the short run, cost containment boosts insurers' profits. In the long run, higher medical costs drive premium prices up. Thus, patients would ultimately pay for increases in service or reimbursements.

Managed care has not stopped the upward spiral of health care costs. Yet the total elimination of managed care could make a bad situation worse. Meanwhile, insurers who impose extra hurdles or resist paying claims are a continuing source of frustration for patients and their families.

The Malaise of Malpractice

Even the best doctor cannot guarantee a good outcome for every patient. Yet bad outcomes are especially tragic if they result from medical professionals' failure to follow proper procedures. Such mistakes can kill patients or leave them severely disabled. Not only do these tragedies affect the patients and their families, but they also shake the community's confidence in the medical profession.

Malpractice is the failure of a professional to follow the applicable standard of care. When physicians commit malpractice, patients can usually sue. The burden of proving malpractice rests with the person bringing the lawsuit, called the plaintiff. If the plaintiff wins, the court generally awards money as damages—amounts meant to compensate for losses caused by the defendant's wrongdoing.

Often, the awards include costs for extra medical care made necessary by the malpractice. Because medical costs

Prognosis for the Future

THESE DOCTORS LOBBY FOR CHANGES TO STATE MEDICAL MALPRACTICE LAWS AT A 2002 RALLY IN HARRISBURG, PENNSYLVANIA. THE AMERICAN MEDICAL ASSOCIATION AND OTHER GROUPS ARGUE THAT MALPRACTICE CLAIMS AND INSURANCE RATES ARE DRIVING UP MEDICAL EXPENSES AND RESTRICTING AMERICANS' ACCESS TO QUALITY HEALTH CARE.

as a whole have risen, awards for malpractice cases have gone up as well. Beyond this, awards often include an amount to compensate for pain and suffering. Awards also can cover a person's foreseeable economic losses. This might include lost income if a disabled person can no longer work.

National Health Care

Punitive damages, meant to punish a defendant, are generally not appropriate in a medical malpractice lawsuit. However, some state laws allow exceptions for especially awful behavior. Other times, juries have expressed their horror by being extra generous in awarding damages for pain and suffering.

In recent decades, damage payments in malpractice cases have risen dramatically. The median settlement in 1998 was $300,000, versus $1 million in 2004. Median jury awards in 2004 were also around $1 million. However, the average jury award was $4.8 million. By going to trial, defendants run the risk that a jury will find them liable for huge amounts of money.

On the one hand, the threat of high damage awards should help keep incompetent persons from practicing medicine. At the same time, it increases costs for all physicians, even the most qualified doctors.

Medical professionals generally have malpractice insurance to protect against the possibility of expensive lawsuits. Premiums for insurance reflect the general levels of damage awards for various claims. An individual's past performance has some bearing on whether insurers renew policies. However, the area of specialty and geographic locale are major factors affecting the levels of malpractice premiums.

Premiums also reflect the legal costs involved in defending against malpractice claims. The defendants' insurers must still pay for lawyers and experts even if a plaintiff loses a case. Average costs for a successful malpractice defense came to $93,559 in 2004.

Groups like the American Tort Reform Association and the American Medical Association say that malpractice insurance costs are substantial, and in some cases, prohibitive. Between 2000 and 2002, average malpractice premiums for all physicians in the United States rose by 15 percent. That was twice the rate of health care spending

Prognosis for the Future

per person. Some specialty areas had even higher increases. Malpractice insurance rates for obstetrician/gynecologists (OB/GYNs) rose 22 percent. Rates for internists and general surgeons went up 33 percent.

Critics of the medical malpractice system say it adds between $60 billion and $100 billion to America's annual health care costs. However, the Congressional Budget Office and the Kaiser Family Foundation report that malpractice insurance costs make up less than 2 percent of America's total health spending. Moreover, one can argue that premiums are not too high if insurers really need those amounts to cover malpractice claims.

Rising malpractice costs may also lead to defensive medicine. In other words, health care providers may order expensive diagnostic tests and other procedures to cover their bases in case patients later assert malpractice claims.

In one sense, erring on the side of caution is a good thing. Tests and other procedures can save lives when they detect serious conditions that a doctor might otherwise miss. From that perspective, it makes little sense to debate defensive medicine when extra procedures may provide medical benefits.

On the other hand, high-tech tests and procedures have been a factor driving up the costs of medical care. Tests that have only slight usefulness may increase patients' costs needlessly. The AMA argues that defensive medicine costs Americans $70 to $267 billion per year.

Groups that want tort limits say that such caps on damages help reduce medical costs. Others argue that the medical profession has a profit incentive for ordering extra tests anyway. Study results are conflicting, so this remains an open question.

In extreme cases, high malpractice premiums might discourage physicians from entering or remaining in certain fields. This, in turn, can limit patients' access to quality health care. For example, rising medical malpractice

National Health Care

costs caused neurosurgeon Chris Heffner to stop treating head trauma patients. At the time, only one other neurosurgeon was practicing south of Springfield in Illinois.

Malpractice insurance has especially affected OB/GYNs. Errors in delivering babies can cause developmental defects that impact children and families for life. Other errors can affect women's future ability to deliver healthy children, or leave them subject to other diseases. In Cleveland, Ohio, OB/GYN malpractice rates more than doubled from 2000 to 2004. For the same period, premiums in Chicago and Miami rose more than 150 percent.

High malpractice premiums have caused some OB/GYNs and other specialists to relocate or to stop performing high-risk procedures. Such moves limit physicians' liability exposure. However, patients may have little or no access to necessary services near their homes. People in high-risk situations may find it especially hard to get the care they need. In an AMA survey, more than a quarter of the doctors surveyed said they had stopped performing certain services during the preceding year. Nearly all in that group cited malpractice concerns as a factor in their decisions.

Because of such problems, various advocates, including President George W. Bush, have called for changes to medical malpractice law. As of 2007, Congress had not passed federal legislation dealing with the issue. However, approximately thirty states have passed laws to change how courts treat medical malpractice claims.

State medical malpractice reforms vary. Some states limit total damage awards. Others limit awards for pain and suffering and other noneconomic damages. Some state laws also limit the share of liability that any defendant might bear. State laws may also shorten the period of time when a plaintiff must begin any lawsuit. Laws may also limit the fees for successful plaintiffs' lawyers or impose penalties for lawsuits that are deemed to be frivolous.

Prognosis for the Future

Gauging the success of such laws is difficult at best. In one study, tort law changes as a whole explained only 7 percent of the variations among states in premiums for malpractice insurance. However, certain law changes had more substantial results. For example, stricter standards on expert witness testimony consistently lowered damage awards. Higher penalties on frivolous lawsuits also had some positive effects. Prohibiting plaintiffs from requesting a specific, high amount of damages at the outset also seemed to limit awards and settlements.

Nonetheless, it remains difficult to judge tort reform efforts. Even if total payouts went down, nothing would force malpractice insurers to pass all savings on to physicians and hospitals. Likewise, health care providers may not respond for a long time to any such changes.

Meanwhile, plaintiffs' lawyers maintain that states should not protect potentially incompetent doctors or limit victims' recovery. The plaintiffs' bar has a strong political voice, through the American Association for Justice and similar groups.

Moreover, medical malpractice claims often evoke sympathy and strong emotional responses from the public. Statistics suggest that medical malpractice may cause up to 100,000 deaths each year. One study showed evidence of negligence and injury for about one out of every hundred hospital patients. No one wants to be that person. And no one wants to see a loved one suffer as a result of malpractice. Thus, the public is loath to limit patients' avenues for recourse.

Equal Access to Healthy Outcomes

The Declaration of Independence says that all men are created equal, and the Constitution guarantees everyone equal protection under the law. Throughout its history,

National Health Care

however, the United States has faced issues of racial and ethnic inequality. This is true in the field of health care as well.

White Americans have long had an advantage over blacks and other ethnic minorities in getting quality health care. Socioeconomic factors explain a large part of the difference. People who are poorer and less educated are less likely to seek and get medical care. At the same time, they are more likely to be in situations or to make decisions that present significant health risks for themselves or their children.

Such inequalities will likely continue as long as any racial groups lag behind in income, education, and other socioeconomic measures. For example, people with low incomes are less likely to have job-based health insurance or to be able to buy coverage on their own. To the extent that minorities are overrepresented in that group, they will make up a larger share of people who cannot afford health care.

Even among people with similar incomes and insurance coverage, though, racial and ethnic disparities in health persist. Forecasters predict that during the coming decades the percentages of various ethnic groups will increase among America's population. This trend heightens the urgency of identifying and dealing with such disparities.

For example, one study found that older black patients were less likely than whites to have their blood sugar, blood pressure, and cholesterol levels under control, despite participation in high-quality Medicare plans. "The data clearly show that even high-performing plans do not provide effective medical treatment to all people," said study coauthor Amal Trivedi of Brown University. "If we improve quality and eliminate disparities, we will save lives." In 2000, the rate of deaths from cardiovascular

Prognosis for the Future

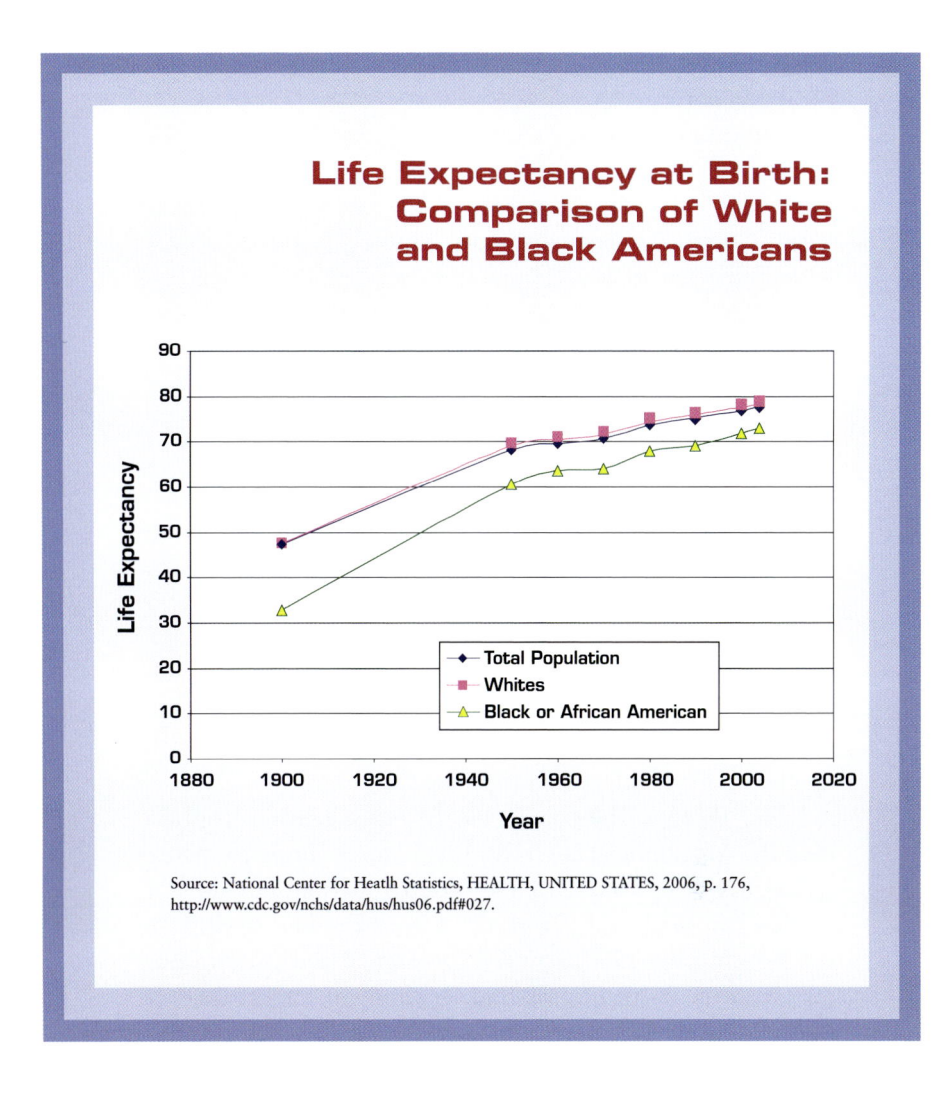

Life Expectancy at Birth: Comparison of White and Black Americans

[Chart showing life expectancy from 1900 to ~2005 for Total Population, Whites, and Black or African American groups]

Source: National Center for Heatlh Statistics, HEALTH, UNITED STATES, 2006, p. 176, http://www.cdc.gov/nchs/data/hus/hus06.pdf#027.

disease was 29 percent higher for blacks than for whites.

No one is certain how best to deal with the problem. Improving equal opportunities throughout society will help eliminate differences caused by varying income and education levels. Beyond that, some health care providers and insurers are stressing greater training in cultural diversity.

Community-based programs may also help meet the needs of people of color, by bringing services to settings where patients will more readily use them. "You would focus in on cultural differences and lifestyles," notes Meredith King of the Center for American Progress, "so that you see better outcomes."

Moving Ahead

Advocates on both ends of the political spectrum say the time for change is now. Yet the political system has much built-in resistance to change. This was one reason behind the failure of the first Clinton health plan during the 1990s.

Moreover, as long as both major political parties have significant representation in the federal government, it will be difficult to make major changes in national health care policy. Recent battles over government-funded health insurance for children demonstrate this.

The State Children's Health Insurance Program (SCHIP, pronounced S-CHIP) gives states funds to insure children whose families have modest income but do not qualify for Medicaid. Congress passed the law setting up the program in 1997, toward the end of the Clinton administration. Both houses had Republican majorities, yet the bill had wide bipartisan support. The law helped children in low-income working families, and it represented a relatively small change in health care policy.

Under the SCHIP law, states can expand Medicaid eligibility limits, run separate programs, or do a combination of the two. By 2006, more than 6.1 million children had benefited from SCHIP, with more than 4 million enrolled at various times. As a result, the percentage of

Prognosis for the Future

THESE CHILDREN AND THEIR PARENTS DEMONSTRATED OUTSIDE THE WHITE HOUSE IN 2007 TO PROTEST PRESIDENT GEORGE W. BUSH'S ANNOUNCEMENT THAT HE WOULD VETO A LAW EXPANDING SCHIP, THE STATE CHILDREN'S HEALTH INSURANCE PROGRAM. CONGRESS FAILED TO OVERRIDE BUSH'S 2007 VETO.

uninsured children fell from 13.5 percent in 1997 to 9.7 percent in 2005.

Unfortunately, about 9 million children remained uninsured in 2007. Most of them would be eligible for either Medicaid or SCHIP. Yet hassles in getting benefits, lack of information, and other barriers stand in the way of full participation. Even when SCHIP covers children, parents often go without health insurance, which leaves families vulnerable. Various states have also had problems funding the program.

When reauthorization came up for debate in 2007, estimates projected a need for another $39 billion over five years to maintain current programs, or about $8 billion a year. Some policy makers wanted to expand the program by funding it with $10 billion per year for five years. Almost all children could have insurance then. This would be clearer because coverage wouldn't be automatic and there would still be eligibility requirements.

Opponents, including President Bush, called for a more scaled-back program. The president wanted to limit increases to $5 billion per year—less than the amount needed for current enrollment. Bush objected to the possibility that some families might switch from private insurance to SCHIP. He also wanted to see changes made through tax incentives, rather than via government grants.

Other critics feared that the program's expansion could turn it into a middle-class entitlement. A *Wall Street Journal* editorial noted that a 2007 proposal by Senator Hillary Clinton (D-NY) would have raised SCHIP eligibility to 400 percent of the federal poverty level. This would have allowed some families earning more than $80,000 per year to benefit from SCHIP. That group is much different from the struggling working families the program was set up to help.

In September 2007 Congress passed a bill to expand SCHIP funding by $35 billion over five years. Although forty-five Republicans in the House of Representatives voted for the bill, President Bush vetoed the measure.

Prognosis for the Future

Meanwhile, eight states filed lawsuits challenging stricter federal rules for SCHIP eligibility. Proponents will continue to push for an expanded program, and SCHIP will likely be an issue beyond the 2008 elections.

The struggle over SCHIP is small compared with the political furor that will result from any major proposal for national health care. Several contenders for the Democratic presidential nomination offered health care reform plans in 2007. Hillary Clinton, Barack Obama, and John Edwards all pushed for universal health care through public-private plans.

All three candidates would require employers to provide health insurance for employees or make other payments so individuals could get insurance. Clinton's plan would help small businesses pay for such insurance. Obama and Edwards would exclude some small businesses.

In any case, Clinton and Edwards would require all individuals to have insurance coverage. Obama's plan stopped short of an individual mandate, but it would cover all children. To help people afford coverage, Clinton, Obama, and Edwards would expand Medicaid and SCHIP. Other individuals might offset their costs for premiums with tax credits or through other incentives.

For all three candidates, the goal would be universal coverage. Toward that end, they would require insurance companies to offer coverage for everyone, even people who cannot now get coverage because of preexisting conditions.

Cost estimates for the programs proposed by these three Democratic candidates ranged from $100 billion to $200 billion per year. Preventive care and greater efficiency would offset part of those costs. Candidates would offset other costs by increasing taxes on higher-income people.

Nevertheless, cost estimates are uncertain at best. Price

National Health Care

DEMOCRATIC PRESIDENTIAL HOPEFUL BARACK OBAMA VISITS AN IOWA RESEARCH LAB WHILE ON THE CAMPAIGN TRAIL IN 2007. HEALTH CARE PLANS PROPOSED BY THE DEMOCRATIC PRESIDENTIAL CANDIDATES WOULD EXPAND HEALTH INSURANCE COVERAGE THROUGH A COMBINATION OF PUBLIC AND PRIVATE INSURANCE PROGRAMS. BUSINESSES AND HIGH-INCOME TAXPAYERS WOULD BEAR THE BIGGEST SHARES OF THE INCREASED COSTS.

could become the major point against universal health coverage plans. Even if Democrats were to control both Congress and the White House, some vested interests in business and insurance would almost surely oppose plans for universal health coverage.

Prognosis for the Future

Contenders for the Republican presidential nomination were less likely to call for universal coverage. Former Massachusetts governor Mitt Romney helped establish his state's program for mandatory coverage. Yet as a presidential candidate, he backed off from individual mandates at the national level. Instead, Romney argued for promoting a better insurance market through tax breaks and streamlined regulations. States would remain free to adopt various reforms as they saw fit.

Another Republican candidate, former New York mayor Rudy Giuliani, called for a shift away from the current system of employer-based insurance. In his view, developing a better market for individuals to buy their own health insurance would result in more consumer choice and greater personal responsibility for health decisions. Among other things, Giuliani would allow a nationwide market for individual insurance, limit medical malpractice claims, and promote health savings accounts.

Arizona Senator John McCain, another candidate for the Republican presidential nomination, focused on the spiraling costs of health care. "Unless you do something about cost, you are chasing your proverbial tail," McCain said in a 2007 speech. He proposed giving low-income families tax credits up to $5,000 to offset the costs of health insurance.

In any case, change in the United States' health care system will involve significant debate. In the meantime, most people have cause for concern about health in the United States. In one study using 2005 data, at least 57 percent of adults in all ethnic groups except Asian and Pacific Americans were overweight or obese. "If you reduce obesity to the 1980 levels," notes Meredith King at CAP, "then you would save at least one $1 trillion dollars over twenty-five years of Medicare."

Aside from treatment costs, reducing obesity levels could boost the country's economic output by more than

National Health Care

$254 billion as early as 2023, reported a study by the Milken Institute, an economics research group in California. This holds true in other areas too. The Milken Institute report noted that preventive care can drastically cut the incidence of common diseases, such as diabetes, hypertension, heart disease, some cancers, and some mental disorders. Savings from effective preventive care programs could save more than $1 trillion per year.

If the United States does not rein in the rates of those diseases, they could cost the economy $6 trillion annually by the middle of this century. However, people who cannot afford medical care are less able to take part in preventive health programs. The country as a whole will eventually bear the cost.

Of course, the national health care debate is not just about money. Few people want to see sick or injured patients suffer. Advocates in both political parties sympathize with people who cannot afford health care and health insurance. They all want the United States to enjoy better health and less hardship.

However, policy makers disagree about the most effective ways to solve present problems and provide health care in the United States. Moreover, health care is just one of many issues that policy makers debate. The United States is a wealthy country, yet its resources have limits. Ultimately, health care must compete with other public needs for limited resources in the economy and in the government budget.

Nearly a century has passed since Theodore Roosevelt observed that when the needs of sick and injured people "are not met by given establishments…, the workers are in jeopardy, the progressive employer is penalized, and the community pays a heavy cost in lessened efficiency and in misery." Critics of America's health care system say that is true now more than ever.

Prognosis for the Future

All proposals come with costs, concerns, and political risks. The main questions are how our democracy should change its health care system, who will pay the costs of any changes, and how those changes will affect the health of all Americans.

Notes

Chapter 1

p. 7, par. 1–3, David Lazarus, "Uninsured Patient Billed More than $12,000 for Broken Rib," *San Francisco Chronicle*, March 30, 2007, p. C1.

p. 7, par. 4–p. 8, par. 1, PBS, "Healthcare Crisis: Who's at Risk? Program Transcript," 2000, http://www.pbs.org/healthcarecrisis/transcript.html (accessed May 2, 2007).

p. 8, par. 6, Dianne Williamson, "How Not to Cut Costs in Health Care: Insurer Opts for Costlier, Less Efficient Procedure," *Sunday Telegram* (Worcester, MA), April 29, 2007, p. B1.

p. 9, par. 3, United States Census Bureau, Current Population Reports, P60-233, *Income, Poverty, and Health Insurance Coverage in the United States: 2006*, pp. 18–19 (Washington, D.C.: U.S. Government Printing Office, 2007), http://www.census.gov/prod/2007pubs/p60-233.pdf (accessed September 27, 2007); Kaiser Family Foundation, "Health Insurance Premium Growth Moderates Slightly in 2006, But Still Increases Twice as Fast as Wages and Inflation," September 26, 2006, http://www.kff.org/insurance/ehbs092606nr.cfm (accessed November 16, 2007).

Notes

p. 13, par. 3, NH Health Cost, "A Deeper Explanation," undated, http://www.nhhealthcost.org/deeperExplanation.aspx (accessed September 27, 2007).

p. 13, par. 5, Richard Wolf, "Study: Uninsured Kids Fare Worse at Hospitals," *USA Today*, March 2, 2007, p. 2A.

p. 15, par. 3, Centers for Medicare & Medicaid Services, "CMS Releases U.S. Health Spending Estimates Through 2005," January 9, 2007, http://www.cms.hhs.gov/apps/media/press/release.asp?Counter=2069 (accessed May 2, 2007); Kaiser Family Foundation, "Health Care Spending in the United States and OECD Countries," January 2007, http://www.kff.org/insurance/snapshot/chcm010307oth.cfm (accessed May 2, 2007).

p. 15, par. 4, "Healthy-Adjusted Life Expectancy (HALE) from WHO, at Birth and at Age 60, Estimates for 2002, OECD Countries," OECD Health Data 2007, July 2007, http://www.ecosante.fr/OCDEENG/59.html (accessed September 28, 2007); "OECD Health Data 2007: How Does the United States Compare?" 2007, www.oecd.org/dataoecd/46/2/38980580.pdf, accessed September 28, 2007; *OECD Factbook 2007* (Paris: Organization for Economic Cooperation and Development, 2007), pp. 216–217, http://masetto.sourceoecd.org/pdf/fact2007pdf/11-01-02.pdf (accessed September 28, 2007); World Health Organization, *World Health Statistics 2007*, (Geneva: World Health Organization, 2007), pp. 22–30, http://www.who.int/whosis/whostat2007.pdf (accessed September 27, 2007).

p. 15–16, par. 1, Health Data 2007, accessed through http://masetto.sourceoecd.org/vl=5178763/cl=25/nw=1/rpsv/statistic/s37_about.htm?jnlissn=99991012 (accessed September 28, 2007); World Health Organization, "World Health Organization Assesses the World's Health Systems," 2000, http://www.who.int/whr/2000/media_centre/press_release/en/index.html (accessed May 2, 2007).

p. 16, par. 2, Commonwealth Fund Commission on a High Performance Health System, "Why Not the Best? Results from a National Scorecard on U.S. Health System Performance," 2006, http://www.commonwealthfund.org/usr_doc/Commission_whynotthebest_951.pdf (accessed September 27, 2007).

National Health Care

p. 16, par. 3, *Income, Poverty, and Health Insurance Coverage in the United States: 2006*, pp. 18–19; Center for American Progress, "Health Care by the Numbers," May 3, 2007, http://www.americanprogress.org/issues/2007/05/health_numbers.html (accessed May 17, 2007); Bloomberg News, "Report: Costs Keep Women from Care," *Newsday*, Nassau/Suffolk ed., April 20, 2007, p. A42; Cathy Schoen, et al., "Insured But Not Protected: How Many Adults Are Underinsured?" *Health Affairs*, Web Exclusive, June 14, 2005, pp. W5–289–W5–302, http://content.healthaffairs.org/cgi/reprint/hlthaff.w5.289v1?ijkey=1hR6oh4Hhh2jc&keytype=ref&siteid=healthaff (accessed May 17, 2007).

p. 16, par. 4, Reuters, "One-third of U.S. Lacked Health Insurance: Survey," ABC News, September 20, 2007, http://abcnews.go.com/US/wireStory?id=3632621(accessed October 1, 2007).

p. 16, par. 5, National Coalition on Health Care, "Health Insurance Cost," 2007, http://www.nchc.org/facts/cost.shtml (accessed May 2, 2007). See also Ezra Klein, "Going Universal," *Los Angeles Times*, December 26, 2006, p. A35.

p. 17, par. 1, Centers for Medicare & Medicaid, "National Health Expenditures Projections, 2006–2016," 2007, Table 1, http://www.cms.hhs.gov/NationalHealthExpendData/downloads/proj2006.pdf (accessed May 2, 2007).

p. 17, par. 5, Catherine Arnst, "Health Care for All? Not Quite," *Business Week*, April 16, 2007, pp. 62–64.

p. 19, par. 2, James Watson, telephone interview with author, June 27, 2007.

p. 19, par. 3, *Retail Industry Leaders Association v. Fielder*, 475 F3d 180 (4th Cir., 2007).

pp. 20–21, sidebar, Sonya Geis and Christopher Lee, "Schwarzenegger Proposes Universal Health Coverage: California Plan Could Cost State $12 Billion," *Washington Post*, January 9, 2007, p. A3.

Chapter 2

p. 24, par. 1, PR Newswire, "New Survey Finds Troubling Data on American Asthma Sufferers," May 15, 2007, http://www.pr-inside.com/new-survey-finds-troubling-data-on-r124494.htm (accessed May 15, 2007); National

Notes

Diabetes Information Clearinghouse, "National Diabetes Statistics," November 2005, http://diabetes.niddk.nih.gov/dm/pubs/statistics/#7 (accessed May 15, 2007).

p. 25, par. 2, American Heart Association, "High Blood Pressure Statistics," 2007, http://www.americanheart.org presenter.jhtml?identifier=4621(accessed May 15, 2007); American Heart Association, "Cholesterol Statistics," 2007, http://www.americanheart.org/presenter.jhtml?identifier=4506 (accessed May 15, 2007).

p. 26, par. 2, "Soaring Drug Costs: A $100,000-a-Year Cancer Treatment," *The Record* (Bergen County, NJ), February 24, 2006, p. L8.

p. 26, par. 4, Agency for Healthcare Research and Quality, "2004 National Statistics," calculated from "National and Regional Statistics from the NIS," http://hcupnet.ahrq.gov/HCUPnet.jsp (accessed May 15, 2007); Anne Elixhauser, et al., "Hospitalization in the United States, 1997: HCUP Fact Book No. 1 (continued)," Agency for Healthcare Research and Quality, 2000, http://www.ahrq.gov/data/hcup/factbk1/fctbk1.htm (accessed May 15, 2007).

p. 27, par. 2, Christopher Rowland, "State OK's Medical Scanners, Renews Cost Debate," *Boston Globe*, April 19, 2006, http://www.boston.com/business/globe/articles/2006/04/19/state_oks_medical_scanners_renews_cost_debate/ (accessed October 2, 2007).

p. 27, par. 3, Ron Winslow, "The Price of a Broken Heart," *Wall Street Journal*, November 5, 2005, p. A1.

p. 27, par. 4, Paul C. Nagle and Abigail W. Smith, "Review of Recent US Cost Estimates of Revascularization," *American Journal of Managed Care*, October 2004, pp. S370–S376, http://www.ajmc.com/Article.cfm?Menu=1&ID=2733 (accessed October 2, 2007).

p. 27, par. 5, James Mehring and Gene Koretz, "Health Care: How Good?" *Business Week*, February 16, 2004, p. 28; Milt Freudenheim, "Latest Medical Devices Bring Bigger Bills," *New York Times*, April 9, 1999, p. C1.

p. 28, par. 4, WebMD, "AARP: Prescription Drug Prices Soaring," March 8, 2007, http://www.cbsnews.com/stories/2007/03/08/health/webmd/main2547741.shtml (accessed May 16, 2007).

p. 28, par. 5, Families USA, "New Report Shows Prices for Top

Medicare Part D Drugs Grew by 9.2 Percent in Last Year," April 18, 2007, http://www.familiesusa.org/resources/newsroom/press-releases/2007-press-releases/new-report-shows-prices-for.html (accessed May 17, 2007).

p. 29, par. 3, "PhRMA Statement on Patent Reform Legislation," April 18, 2007, http://www.phrma.org/news_room/press_releases/phrma_statement_on_patent_reform_legislation/ (accessed May 16, 2007); see also Pharmaceutical Research and Manufacturers of America, "Reporters Handbook," http://www.phrma.org/key_industry_facts_about_phrma/ (accessed May 16, 2007).

p. 29, par. 5, Steven Projan, M.D., telephone interview with author, August 6, 2004; cf. Jacob Sullum, "Exporting Drug Prices," *Reason*, May 2007, pp. 10–11.

pp. 29–30, par. 1, Henry A. Waxman, "Pharmaceutical Industry Profits Increase by Over $8 Billion After Medicare Drug Plan Goes into Effect," September 2006, http://oversight.house.gov/Documents/20060919115623-70677.pdf (accessed June 27, 2007).

p. 30, par. 2, James M. Hoffman, et al., "Projecting Future Drug Expenditures—2007," *American Journal of Health-System Pharmacy*, February 1, 2007, pp. 298–314.

p. 30–31, Partnership for Prescription Assistance, undated, https://www.pparx.org/Intro.php (accessed May 25, 2007).

p. 32, sidebar, Conference call with Debbie Stabenow, Dean Baker, and Roger Hickey, arranged by Campaign for America's Future, April 4, 2007; see also Diana Manos, "Senate Blunts Democrat Push for Federal Negotiation of Prescription Drug Prices," Healthcare Finance News, April 18, 2007, http://www.healthcarefinancenews.com/story.cms?id=6369 (accessed November 16, 2007).

p. 33, par. 3, David Glendinning, "Annual Medicare Trustees Report Issues Dire Forecast for Part B," *American Medical News*, May 14, 2007, http://www.ama-assn.org/amednews/2007/05/14/gvl10514.htm (accessed June 25, 2007); Thomas R. Saving, "Medicare Meltdown, *Wall Street Journal*, May 9, 2007, p. A17; "Medicare's Troubling Prospects," *New York Times*, April 26, 2007, p. A24.

p. 34, par. 4, Bureau of Labor Statistics, "Employee Tenure Summary," September 8, 2006, http://www.bls.gov/news

Notes

.release/tenure.nr0.htm (accessed May 10, 2007); United States Census Bureau, Current Population Survey, "Employee Tenure in the Mid-1990s," January 30, 1997, http://www.bls.census.gov/cps/pub/tenure_0296.htm (accessed May 15, 2007).

pp. 34–35, United States Bureau of the Census, "Income and Job Mobility in the Early 1990s," February 1995, http://www.census.gov/apsd/www/statbrief/sb95_1.pdf (accessed May 10, 2007); Office of the White House, "Address of the President to the Joint Session of Congress," September 22, 1993, www.ibiblio.org/nhs/supporting/remarks-final.html (accessed January 24, 2007).

p. 35, par. 2, Congressional Budget Office, "What Accounts for the Decline in Manufacturing Employment?" February 18, 2004, http://www.cbo.gov/ftpdoc.cfm?index=5078&type=0&sequence=0 (accessed May 10, 2007); cf. Josh Bivens, "Shifting Blame for Manufacturing Job Loss," Economic Policy Institute, April 8, 2004, http://www.epinet.org/content.cfm/briefingpapers_bp149 (accessed May 10, 2007).

p. 35, par. 3, Susan Starr Sered and Rushika Fernandopulle, *Uninsured in America: Life & Death in the Land of Opportunity* (Berkeley: University of California Press, 2005), pp. 27–28.

pp. 35–36, Sered and Fernandopulle, pp. 44–45.

p. 36, par. 2, Jonathan Cohn, *Sick: The Untold Story of America's Health Care Crisis—and the People Who Pay the Price* (New York: HarperCollins Publishers, 2007), p. 10.

p. 36, par. 3–4, Bureau of Labor Statistics, "Employed Persons by Sex, Occupation, Class of Worker, Full- or Part-time Status, and Race," 2007, http://www.bls.gov/cps/cpsaat12.pdf (accessed May 10, 2007); Bureau of Labor Statistics, "Contingent and Alternative Employment Arrangements, February 2005," July 27, 2005, http://www.bls.gov/news.release/conemp.nr0.htm (accessed May 10, 2007).

p. 38, par. 2, Julie Appleby, "Health Insurance Costs Rise 7.7%, Twice the Rate of Inflation," USAToday.com, September 27, 2006, http://www.usatoday.com/money/industries/health/2006-09-26-health-premiums_x.htm (accessed October 1, 2007).

p. 39, par. 2, Kaiser Family Foundation, "Health Insurance

Premium Growth Moderates Slightly in 2006, But Still Increases Twice as Fast as Wages and Inflation," September 26, 2006, http://www.kff.org/insurance/ehbs092606nr.cfm (accessed May 15, 2007); see also Kathleen Kingsbury, "Pressure on Your Health Benefits," *Time*, November 6, 2006, p. 53.

p. 39, par. 3, Conference call with Tom Daschle, Karen Davenport, and Meena Seshamani, arranged by Center for American Progress, April 12, 2007.

p. 39, par. 4, John A. Graves and Sharon K. Long, "Why Do People Lack Health Insurance?" Urban Institute, May 22, 2006, http://www.urban.org/UploadedPDF/411317_lack_health_ins.pdf (accessed May 15, 2007); see also Sara R. Collins, et al, "On the Edge: Low-Wage Workers and Their Health Insurance Coverage," Commonwealth Fund Issue Brief, April 2003, http://www.commonwealthfund.org/usr_doc/collins_ontheedge_ib_626.pdf (accessed May 15, 2007).

p. 39, par. 5, J. Edward Hill, "Ethical Issues in Health Care: Communicating and Persuading and Training," *Vital Speeches of the Day*, March 2007, pp. 127, 128.

p. 40, par. 1, Kaiser Family Foundation, "Health Insurance Premium Growth Moderates Slightly in 2006, But Still Increases Twice as Fast as Wages and Inflation," September 26, 2007, http://www.kff.org/insurance/ehbs092606nr.cfm (accessed May 15, 2007).

p. 40, par. 2, Telephone conference call with Tom Daschle and Karen Davenport and Meena Seshamani, arranged by Center for American Progress, April 12, 2007.

p. 40, par. 4, "After Sorry 14-year Hiatus, Health-care Debate Revives," *USA Today*, February 26, 2007, p. 10A.

pp. 40–41, Better Health Care Together, "AT&T, Baker Center, Center for American Progress, CED, CWA, Intel, Kelly Services, SEIU and Wal-Mart Launch 'Better Health Care Together' Campaign," February 7, 2007, http://phx.corporate-ir.net/phoenix.zhtml?c=113058&p=irol-newsArticle&ID=960781&highlight= (accessed June 13, 2007).

Chapter 3

p. 44, par. 1, Andrew H. Beck, "The Flexner Report and the Standardization of American Medical Education," *JAMA:*

Notes

The Journal of the American Medical Association, May 5, 2004, pp. 2139–2140.

pp. 44–45, Theodore Roosevelt, "Acceptance Speech at the National Convention of the Progressive Party," August 6, 1912, reprinted in Mario R. Dinunzio, *Theodore Roosevelt* (Washington, DC: CQ Press, 2003), pp. 291–297, at p. 295.

p. 45, par. 3–5, Forrest A. Walker, "Compulsory Health Insurance: 'The Next Great Step in Social Legislation,'" *Journal of American History*, September 1969, pp. 290 (accessed through *JSTOR*, May 7, 2007); *see also* Aaron Steelman, "If Only Samuel Gompers Were Alive Today," October 28, 1996, http://www.cato.org/pub_display.php?pub_id=6274 (accessed November 11, 2007).

p. 46, par. 3, *Medical Care for the American People: The Final Report of the Committee on the Costs of Medical Care* (Chicago: University of Chicago Press, 1932; reprinted Washington, D.C.: U.S. Department of Health, Education, and Welfare, 1970), pp. xxvi, 120.

pp. 46–47, Julius B. Richmond and Rashi Fein, *The Health Care Mess: How We Got Into It and What It Will Take To Get Out* (Cambridge, MA: Harvard University Press, 2005), p. 14; Jonathan Engel, *Doctors and Reformers: Discussion and Debate over Health Policy, 1925–1950* (Columbia: University of South Carolina Press, 2002), p. 43.

p. 49, par. 2, J.F. Follman, Jr., "The Growth of Group Health Insurance," *Journal of Risk and Insurance*, March 1965, pp. 105–112, at p. 105 (accessed through *JSTOR*, May 7, 2007).

p. 49, par. 4, Jacob S. Hacker, *The Great Risk Shift: The Assault on American Jobs, Families, Health Care, and Retirement and How You Can Fight Back* (New York: Oxford University Press, 2006), p. 145; Richmond and Fein, *The Health Care Mess*, pp. 37–38; Laura D. Hermer, "Private Health Insurance in the United States: A Proposal for a More Functional System," *Houston Journal of Health Law and Policy*, Fall 2005, pp 1, 10–11; Engel, *Doctors and Reformers*, p. 317.

p. 50, par. 2, Harry S. Truman, "Special Message to Congress Recommending a Comprehensive Health Program,"

National Health Care

November 19, 1945, http://www.trumanlibrary.org/public papers/index.php?pid=483&st=&st1= (accessed May 8, 2007).

p. 51, par. 2, Lyndon Baines Johnson, "Remarks in New York City Before the 50th Anniversary Convention of the Amalgamated Clothing Workers—May 9, 1964," excerpted at Centers for Medicare & Medicaid Services, "CMS History Project—President's Speeches," undated, pp. 6–7, http://www.cms.hhs.gov/History/Downloads/CMSPresidents Speeches.pdf (accessed May 9, 2007).

pp. 52–53, sidebar, Truman.

p. 55, par. 2–3, Richard Nixon, "Special Message to Congress on Health Care," March 2, 1972, excerpted in Centers for Medicare & Medicaid Services, "CMS History Project—President's Speeches," undated, pp. 52–69, http://www.cms.hhs.gov/History/Downloads/CMSPresidentsSpeeches.pdf (accessed May 9, 2007); see also Katharine R. Levit, et al., "National Health Spending Trends, 1960–1993," *Health Affairs*, Winter 1994, pp. 14, 15.

p. 58, par. 5, Jimmy Carter, "National Health Plan Remarks Announcing Proposed Legislation," June 12, 1979, http://www.presidency.ucsb.edu/ws/index.php?pid=32465&st=health+care&st1= (accessed May 16, 2007).

p. 59, Office of the White House, "Address of the President to the Joint Session of Congress," September 22, 1993, www.ibiblio.org/nhs/supporting/remarks-final.html (accessed January 24, 2007); "Excerpts from Clinton's Remarks: Clinton's Health Care Plan," *Boston Globe*, September 23, 1993, National/Foreign, p. 14.

p. 61, par. 2, Dana Priest and Fern Shen, "Health Plan Costly for Many; Officials Estimate 40 Percent To Pay More," *Washington Post*, October 29, 1993, p. A1; Senate Finance Committee, "Hearing Re: Health Care Reform," October 28, 1993 (accessed through Lexis/Nexis Congressional Publications, June 14, 2007).

p. 61, par. 4, Craig Weil, "Do We Really Want Politicians To Control Health Care in America?" *Atlanta Journal and Constitution*, November 5, 1993, p. A15.

pp. 61–62, par. 1, PBS, "A Detailed Timeline of the Healthcare Debate Portrayed in 'The System,'" 1996, http://www.pbs.org/newshour/forum/may96/background/health_debate_page2.html (accessed June 14, 2007); "Health Care Re-

Notes

form Today," November 14, 1993, http://www.ibiblio.org/darlene/reform/11493-reform.html (accessed June 14, 2007).

p. 62, par. 4, Robert J. Blendon, Mollyann Brodie, and John Benson, "What Happened to Americans' Support for the Clinton Health Plan?" *Health Affairs*, Summer 1995, pp. 7, 8, http://content.healthaffairs.org/cgi/reprint/14/2/7.pdf (accessed June 14, 2007).

Chapter 4

p. 66, par. 3, Sue Blevins, "Restoring Health Freedom: The Case for a Universal Tax Credit for Health Insurance," Cato Institute, December 12, 1997, pp. 4–5, http://www.cato.org/pubs/pas/pa-290.pdf (accessed June 18, 2007).

p. 68, par. 6, Healthy & Wealthy: Health Savings Accounts Offer Lower Health Insurance Costs and Greater Consumer Control; Are They Right for You?" *Minnesota Technology*, Summer 2006, http://www.minnesotatechnology.org/publications/magazine/2006/Summer/HealthyWealthy.asp (accessed May 28, 2007).

p. 69, par. 4, Office of the White House, "President Participates in Conversation on Health Care," January 26, 2005, http://www.whitehouse.gov/news/releases/2005/01/20050126-5.html (accessed May 28, 2007); Michael A. Fletcher, "Bush Promotes Health Savings Accounts," *Washington Post*, January 27, 2005, p. A2.

pp. 69–70, par. 1, John W. Snow, "Testimony on the Benefits of Health Savings Accounts (HSAs) Before the Special Committee on Aging, U.S. Senate, May 19, 2004, http://www.treas.gov/press/releases/js1665.htm (accessed May, 28, 2007), reprinted in part at John W. Snow, "Health Savings Accounts: The Debate Over Consumer-Driven Care: PRO," *Congressional Digest*, March 2006, p. 74.

pp. 70–71, par. 2, Office of the White House, "President Bush Participates in Meeting on Health Savings Accounts," April 2, 2007, http://www.whitehouse.gov/news/releases/2007/04/20070402-2.html (accessed May 28, 2007).

p. 71, par. 2, Greg D'Angelo, Heritage Foundation, telephone interview with author, May 31, 2007.

p. 71, par. 4, Families USA, "President's Proposal Would Make Health Care Less, Not More, Affordable," press release, February 15, 2006, http://www.familiesusa.org/resources/

National Health Care

newsroom/statements/2007-statements/Presidents-Proposal-Would-Make.html (accessed June 4, 2007).

pp. 72–73, sidebar, John Dickens, "Health Savings Accounts: Early Enrollee Experiences with Accounts and Eligible Health Plans," Testimony before the Subcommittee on Health Care, Committee on Finance, U.S. Senate, September 26, 2006, http://www.gao.gov/new.items/d061133t.pdf (accessed May 28, 2007).

p. 74, par. 4, Sue Blevins, "Restoring Health Freedom."

p. 75, par. 3, Miller, Matt, "A Good Idea Inside a Bad One," *Time*, February 5, 2007, p. 25 (estimating $200 billion); Heartland Institute, "Why We Need Market-based Health Care Reform: Part 1 of 2," March 1, 2001, http://www.heartland.org/Article.cfm?artId=728 (accessed May 30, 2007) ($125 billion estimate).

pp. 75–76, Office of the White House, "President Bush Delivers State of the Union Address," January 23, 2007, http://www.whitehouse.gov/news/releases/2007/01/20070123-2.html (accessed June 4, 2007).

p. 76, par. 4–5, Families USA, "Bush Health Proposal in State of the Union Message Won't Make Insurance Affordable," January 23, 2007, http://www.familiesusa.org/resources/newsroom/statements/2007-statements/Prez-budget-cuts-2007.html (accessed June 4, 2007).

p. 76, par. 6, Stuart M. Butler and Nina Owcharenko, "Making Health Care Affordable: Bush's Bold Health Tax Reform Plan," Heritage Foundation, January 22, 2007, http://www.heritage.org/Research/HealthCare/wm1316.cfm (accessed May 31, 2007).

p. 78, par. 4, Ronald F. Pollack, "At the Hearing on H.R. 2355, the Health Care Choice Act," June 28, 2005, http://www.familiesusa.org/resources/newsroom/ron-pollack-testimony-health-care-choice-act.html (accessed June 4, 2007).

Chapter 5

pp. 83–84, Institute of Medicine, *Insuring America's Health: Principles and Recommendations* (Washington, D. C.: National Academics Press, 2004), p. 14.

p. 85, par. 2, Thomas C. Kelly, et al., "Health Care Is a Moral Right, a Safeguard of Human Life," December 6, 2005, http://www.ccky.org/Resources/Public%20Witness/Health

Notes

%20Care%20Is%20a%20Moral%20Right.pdf (accessed June 19, 2007); see also Peter Smith, "Catholic Bishops: Health Care a 'Moral Right,'" *Louisville Courier-Journal*, December 8, 2005, http://press.ky.gov/PressClipDetail.asp?REC=180328 (accessed November 17, 2007).

p. 85, par. 3, Risa Lavizzo-Mourey, "Health Care Justice in America: The Moral and Economic Imperatives To Cover the Uninsured," *Vital Speeches of the Day*, June 2007, pp. 261, 262; Institute of Medicine, *Insuring America's Health*, p. 8.

p. 86, par. 5, Roger Hickey, telephone interview with author, April 11, 2007.

p. 87, par. 2, Eric R. Kingson and John M. Cornman, "Health Care Reform: Universal Access Is Feasible and Necessary," *Benefits Quarterly*, Third Quarter 2007, pp. 27, 31; Centers for Disease Control and Prevention, "Fact Sheet: Racial/Ethnic Health Disparities," April 2, 2004, http://www.cdc.gov/od/oc/media/pressrel/fs040402.htm (accessed November 12, 2007).

p. 87, par. 3, Jacob S. Hacker, *The Great Risk Shift: The Assault on American Jobs, Families, Health Care, and Retirement and How You Can Fight Back* (New York: Oxford University Press, 2006), p. 141.

p. 87, par. 4, Senator Tom Daschle, "Living Without Health Insurance: Why Every American Needs Coverage," Testimony before the Subcommittee on Health, Committee on Energy and Commerce, United States House of Representatives, April 25, 2007, http://www.americanprogress.org/issues/2007/04/pdf/daschle_testimony.pdf (accessed November 17, 2007).

pp. 87–88, "Election '08: Talk with the Candidates," WashingtonPost.com, October 18, 2007, http://www.washingtonpost.com/wp-dyn/content/discussion/2007/10/05/DI2007100502319.html (accessed November 17, 2007); Ruy Teixeira, "Public Opinion Snapshot: Universal Health Care Momentum Swells," March 27, 2007, http://www.americanprogress.org/issues/2007/03/opinion_health_care.html (accessed June 23, 2007); Robin Toner, Janet Elder, et al., "Most Support U.S. Guarantee of Health Care," *New York Times*, March 2, 2007, p. A1.

pp. 87–88, par. 1, Jonathan Cohn, *Sick: The Untold Story of America's Health Care Crisis—and the People Who Pay the Price* (New York: HarperCollins Publishers, 2007), p. 231.

p. 89, par. 2, Roger Hickey, telephone interview with author, April 11, 2007.

p. 89, par. 3, Uwe E. Reinhardt, "The Medicare World From Both Sides: A Conversation with Tom Scully," *Health Affairs*, November/December 2003, pp. 167, 170, http://content.healthaffairs.org/cgi/reprint/22/6/167?ck=nck (accessed June 22, 2007).

pp. 89–90, Karen Davenport and Meredith King, telephone interview with author, April 26, 2007.

p. 92, pars. 2–4, David R. Francis, "Michael Moore Refocuses Healthcare Debate," *Christian Science Monitor*, June 18, 2007, p. 15; David Mechanic, *The Truth about Health Care: Why Reform Is Not Working in America* (New Brunswick, NJ: Rutgers University Press, 2006), pp. 174–175.

p. 93, par. 4, Office of Arnold Schwarzenegger, "Governor Schwarzenegger Announces Veto of Government-run Health Care System," September 5, 2006, http://gov.ca.gov/index.php?/press-release/3751 (accessed June 26, 2007); Arnold Schwarzenegger, "I Cannot Support Socialized Medicine," *San Diego Union-Tribune*, September 5, 2006, http://www.signonsandiego.com/uniontrib/20060905/znews_arnold5.html (accessed June 26, 2007).

pp. 93–94, Eddy van Doorslaer, Cristina Masseria, and Xander Koolman, "Inequalities in Access to Medical Care by Income in Developed Countries," *Canadian Medical Association Journal*, January 17, 2006, pp. 177, 181.

p. 95, par. 1, J. Edward Hill, "Ethical Issues in Health Care: Communicating and Persuading and Training," *Vital Speeches of the Day*, March 2007, pp. 127, 129.

p. 95, par. 2, "Michael Moore," *The Daily Show*, June 27, 2007, http://www.comedycentral.com/motherload/player.jhtml?ml_video=89245&ml_collection=&ml_gateway=&ml_gateway_id=&ml_comedian=&ml_runtime=&ml_context=show&ml_origin_url=%2Fmotherload%2F%3Flnk%3Dv%26ml_video%3D89245&ml_playlist=&lnk=&is_large=true (accessed June 28, 2007).

p. 95, par. 4, Amy Finkelstein, "The Cost of Coverage," *Wall Street Journal*, February 28, 2007, p. A14.

Notes

p. 95, par. 5, Diana Ernst, "'Universal' Health Care Could Bankrupt Taxpayers," *Wall Street Journal*, March 7, 2007, p. B12.

pp. 95–96, par. 1, David Whelan, "Is There Another Doctor in the House?" *Forbes*, March 26, 2007, p. 50.

pp. 96–97, par. 1, Jonathan Cohn and David Grazter, "Universal Health Scare," New Republic Online, April 16, 2007, http://www.tnr.com/doc.mhtml?i=w070416&s=cohngratzer041607 (accessed June 24, 2007).

p. 97, par. 2, Michael D. Tanner and Michael F. Cannon, "Universal Healthcare's Dirty Little Secrets," Cato Institute, http://www.cato.org/pub_display.php?pub_id=8172 (accessed June 24, 2007).

p. 97, par. 6, Roger Hickey, telephone interview with author, April 11, 2007.

p. 98, par. 3, Senator Tom Daschle, "Living Without Health Insurance: Why Every American Needs Coverage," Testimony before the Subcommittee on Health, Committee on Energy and Commerce, United States House of Representatives, April 25, 2007, pp. 4–5, http://www.americanprogress.org/issues/2007/04/pdf/daschle_testimony.pdf accessed November 17, 2007).

p. 99, sidebar, par. 1–2, Ann H., personal interview with author, June 23, 2007 (full name withheld upon request to protect patient confidentiality).

p. 99, sidebar, par. 3–4, Mike M., personal interview with author, June 28, 2007, and personal knowledge of the author (full name withheld upon request to protect patient confidentiality).

p. 100, Daschle.

Chapter 6

pp. 102–103, Laura Landro, "Better Ways To Treat Back Pain," *Wall Street Journal*, May 16, 2007, pp. D1, D8 ; National Committee for Quality Assurance, "New HCQA Program Will Recognize Excellence in Caring for Back Pain," January 18, 2007, http://web.ncqa.org/tabid/225/Default.aspx (accessed May 17, 2007); see also American Chiropractic Association, "Medicare: Quality: NCQA's Back Pain Recognition Program (BPRP), undated, http://www.acatoday.org/content_css.cfm?CID=2298 (accessed November 17, 2007).

National Health Care

p. 103, par. 2, Kate Johnson, "Potentially Inappropriate Meds Prescribed for 39% of Managed-care Elderly," *Clinical Psychiatry News*, April 2006, p. 41.

p. 103, par. 3, "Health Plan Errors and Denials Top Consumer Complaints in N.Y.," *Daily Record* (Rochester, NY), March 29, 2006, p. NA (accessed through InfoTrac OneFile, May 21, 2007).

p. 103, par. 4, Susan J. Landers, "Study Highlights Managed Care Conflicts," *American Medical News*, August 16, 1999, p. 5.

pp. 103–04, Jonathan Cohn, *Sick: The Untold Story of America's Health Care Crisis—and the People Who Pay the Price* (New York: HarperCollins Publishers, 2007), pp. 74–75.

p. 104, par. 3, *Aetna Health Inc. v. Davila*, 542 U.S. 200 (2004).

pp. 104–05, "Conn. Bill Seeks To Limit Claim Denials," *Family Practice Management*, April 2007, p. 23.

p. 105, par. 5, Karen Davenport and Meredith King, telephone interview with author, April 26, 2007; *see also* Lori Chordas, "When Consumer-directed Plans Met Managed Care," *Best's Review*, October 2006, p. 78.

p. 108, par. 3, Insurance Information Institute, "Medical Malpractice," May 2007, http://www.iii.org/media/hottopics/insurance/medicalmal/ (accessed May 30, 2007).

pp. 108–109, American Medical Association, "Medical Liability Reform—NOW!" July 19, 2006, http://www.ama-assn.org/ama1/pub/upload/mm/-1/mlrnow.pdf (accessed May 30, 2007); Carolina Gutiérrez and Usha Ranji, "U.S. Health Care Costs: Background Brief," Kaiser Family Foundation, September 2005, http://www.kaiseredu.org/topics_im.asp?imID=1&parentID=61&id=358#5b (accessed May 30, 2007); Richard Tomkins, "Analysis: Bush Pushes Tort Reform," *UPI Perspectives*, January 5, 2005, p. NA (accessed through InfoTrac OneFile, May 23, 2007); Perry Beider and Stuart Hagen, "Limiting Tort Liability for Medical Malpractice," Congressional Budget Office, January 8, 2004, http://www.cbo.gov/ftpdocs/49xx/doc4968/01-08-MedicalMalpractice.pdf (accessed May 30, 2007).

p. 109, American Medical Association, "Medical Liability

Notes

Reform—NOW!"; Tomkins, "Analysis: Bush Pushes Tort Reform;" Beider and Hagan, "Limiting Tort Liability for Medical Malpractice."

p. 110, par. 2, R. W. Hale, "Legal Issues Impacting Women's Access to Care in the United States—The Malpractice Insurance Crisis," *International Journal of Gynecology & Obstetrics*, September 2006, pp. 382, 383, http://www.figo.org/docs/World%20Report%20Pages%20382-385.pdf (accessed May 23, 2007).

p. 110, par. 3, American Medical Association, "Medical Liability Reform—NOW!" But see Beider and Hagan, "Limiting Tort Liability for Medical Malpractice."

pp. 110–111, Teresa M. Waters, et al., "Impact of State Tort Reforms on Physician Malpractice Payments," *Health Affairs*, March/April 2007, pp. 500–509.

p. 111, par. 4, American Association for Justice, "*The Medical Malpractice Myth* by Tom Baker," undated, http://www.atla.org/pressroom/FACTS/health/baker.pdf (accessed May 23, 2007); Tom Baker, *The Medical Malpractice Myth* (Chicago: University of Chicago Press, 2005), pp. 22, 29.

pp. 112–114, Centers for Disease Control and Prevention, "Eliminating Racial & Ethnic Health Disparities," May 11, 2007, http://www.cdc.gov/omh/AboutUs/disparities.htm (accessed June 29, 2007; "Racial Disparities Universal in Medicare Health Plans, Study Finds," Brown University, October 24, 2006, http://www.brown.edu/Administration/News_Bureau/2006-07/06-039.html (accessed June 29, 2007); see also Anne Underwood, "Medicine's Racial Gap," Newsweek Online, October 24, 2006, http://www.msnbc.msn.com/id/15404055/site/newsweek/ (accessed June 29, 2007).

p. 114, par. 2, Meredith King and Karen Davenport, telephone interview with author, April 26, 2007.

pp. 114–116, Vernon Smith, et al., "SCHIP Turns 10: An Update on Enrollment and the Outlook on Reauthorization from the Program's Directors," Kaiser Commission on Medicaid and the Uninsured," May 2007, pp. 5–6, 25, http://www.kff.org/medicaid/upload/7642.pdf (accessed June 25, 2007); Lisa Dubay, Testimony before Senate Finance Committee, Subcommittee on Health, "Hearings on the CHIP Program: From the States' Perspective," November 16, 2006, pp. 4–5, http://ccf.georgetown.edu/pdfs/testimony-Dubay-2.pdf (accessed June 25, 2007).

pp. 115–116, par. 1, Voices for America's Children, "New Plan Must Reach 9 Million Uninsured children," Medical News Today, January 26, 2007, http://www.medicalnewstoday.com/medicalnews.php?newsid=61562 (accessed June 25, 2007).

p. 116, par. 2, Congressional Budget Office, "The State Children's Health Insurance Program," May 2007, p. p. 14, http://www.cbo.gov/ftpdocs/80xx/doc8092/05-10-SCHIP.pdf (accessed June 25, 2007); Conference call with Debbie Stabenow, Dean Baker, and Roger Hickey, arranged by Campaign for America's Future, April 4, 2007.

p. 116, par. 4, SCHIP for Everyone," *Wall Street Journal*, September 28, 2007, p. A14.

pp. 117–118, "If at First You Don't Succeed," *Economist*, September 22, 2007, pp. 40–42; Patrick Healy and Robin Toner, "Wary of Past, Clinton Unveils a Health Plan," *New York Times*, September 18, 2007, p. A1; Anne E. Korblut and Perry Bacon, Jr., "Obama Says Washington Is Ready for Health Plan," *Washington Post*, May 30 2007, p. A5; Jill Lawrence, "Democrats Duel over Health Care," USAToday.com, May 29, 2007, http://www.usatoday.com/news/politics/2007-05-29-democrats-health-care_N.htm (accessed October 3, 2007); Rob Christensen, "Edwards Offers Up a $120 Billion a Year Universal Health Plan," *News & Observer* (Raleigh, NC), February 6, 2007, p. B7.

p. 119, par. 3, Marc Santora, "McCain Health Care Plan Puts Focus on Spending," *New York Times*, October 12, 2007, p. A20.

p. 119, Karen Davenport and Meredith King, telephone interview with author, April 26, 2007; Cara James, et al., "Key Facts: Race, Ethnicity, and Medical Care," Kaiser Family Foundation, January 2007, p. 12, http://www.kff.org/minorityhealth/upload/6069-02.pdf (accessed June 29, 2007).

pp. 119–120, par. 2, Ross DeVrol and Armen Bedroussian, *An Unhealthy America: The Economic Burden of Chronic Disease* (Santa Monica, CA: Milken Institute, October 2007), Sec. 2, p. 2, 22, http://www.milkeninstitute.org/pdf/chronic_disease_report.pdf (accessed November 14,

Notes

2007); Lisa Girion, "Healthy Living Could Save U.S. $1 Trillion, Study Finds," *Los Angeles Times*, October 3, 2007, http://www.latimes.com/business/la-fi-prevent3oct03,1,5741914.story?coll=la-headlines-business&ctrack=1&cset=true (accessed October 3, 2007).

pp. 120–121, Theodore Roosevelt, "Acceptance Speech at the National Convention of the Progressive Party," August 6, 1912, reprinted in Mario R. Dinunzio, *Theodore Roosevelt* (Washington, DC: CQ Press, 2003), pp. 291–297, at p. 295.

Further Information

Further Reading

Bartlett, Donald L., and James B. Steele. *Critical Condition: How Health Care in America Became Big Business—and Bad Medicine.* New York: Doubleday, 2004.

Cohn, Jessica. "What's Up at the Doc's? What You Need To Know about Health Care." *Current Health* 2, November 2006, p. 26.

Cohn, Jonathan. *Sick: The Untold Story of America's Health Care Crisis—And the People Who Pay the Price.* New York: HarperCollins Publishers, 2007.

Geyman, John. *Falling Through the Safety Net: Americans without Health Insurance.* Monroe, ME: Common Courage Press, 2005.

Harris, Nancy, and Helen Cothran, eds. *Does the United States Need a National Health Insurance Policy?* Farmington Hills, MI: Greenhaven Press, 2006.

Further Information

Jonas, Steven. *An Introduction to the U.S. Health Care System*. New York: Springer Pub., 2003.

Tumulty, Karen. "It's Universal." *Time*, April 9, 2007, p. 42.

Organizations and Web Sites

Campaign for America's Future
http://home.ourfuture.org/healthcareforall/

Cato Institute
http://www.cato.org/healthcare/index.html

Center for American Progress
http://www.americanprogress.org/projects/healthprogress/

Center for Economic and Policy Research
http://www.cepr.net

Center for Studying Health System Change
http://www.hschange.com/

Families USA
http://www.familiesusa.org

Heritage Foundation
http://www.heritage.org/research/healthcare/

Kaiser Family Foundation
http://www.kff.org

Progressive Policy Institute
http://www.ppionline.org

Bibliography

Abramson, John. *Overdo$ed America: The Broken Promise of American Medicine.* New York: HarperCollins, 2004.

Albert, Tanya. "Accepting No Deliveries: When Medical Liability Insurance Drives Physicians Out of Rural Mississippi, Pregnant Women Are Left Feeling the Pain." *American Medical News*, September 9, 2002, p. 13.

Alguire, Patrick C. "Understanding Capitation." American College of Physicians, 1996–2007. http://www.acponline.org/counseling/understandcapit.htm (Accessed May 21, 2007).

Andrews, Charles. *Profit Fever: The Drive to Corporatize Health Care and How to Stop It.* Monroe, ME: Common Courage Press, 1995.

Applebaum, Leon. "The Development of Voluntary Health Insurance in the United States," *Journal of Insurance*, September 1961, p. 25 (Accessed through *JSTOR*, May 7, 2007).

Bibliography

Baker, Tom. *The Medical Malpractice Myth*. Chicago: University of Chicago Press, 2005.

Bartlett, Donald L., and James B. Steele. *Critical Condition: How Health Care in America Became Big Business—and Bad Medicine*. New York: Doubleday, 2004.

Beider, Perry, and Stuart Hagen. "Limiting Tort Liability for Medical Malpractice." Congressional Budget Office. January 8, 2004. http://www.cbo.gov/ftpdocs/49xx/doc4968/01-08-MedicalMalpractice.pdf (Accessed May 30, 2007).

Blevins, Sue. "Restoring Health Freedom: The Case for a Universal Tax Credit for Health Insurance." Cato Institute, December 12, 1997. http://www.cato.org/pubs/pas/pa290.pdf (Accessed June 18, 2007).

Bobinski, Mary Ann. "Health Disparities and the Law: Wrongs in Search of a Right." *American Journal of Law & Medicine*, 2003, p. 363.

Butler, Stuart M., and Nina Owcharenko. "Making Health Care Affordable: Bush's Bold Health Tax Reform Plan." Heritage Foundation, January 22, 2007. http://www.heritage.org/Research/HealthCare/wm1316.cfm (Accessed May 31, 2007).

Cannon, Michael F., and Michael D. Tanner. *Healthy Competition: What's Holding Back Health Care and How to Free It*. Washington, DC: Cato Institute, 2005.

Carter, Jimmy. "National Health Plan Message to the Congress on Proposed Legislation." June 12, 1979. http://www.presidency.ucsb.edu/ws/index.php?pid=32466&st=health+care&st1= (Accessed May 16, 2007).

Center for American Progress. "Progressive Prescriptions for a Healthy America." 2005. http://www.americanprogress.org/projects/healthprogress/pdf/prog_prescriptions.pdf (Accessed June 22, 2007).

National Health Care

Centers for Disease Control and Prevention. "Eliminating Racial & Ethnic Health Disparities." June 5, 2007. http://www.cdc.gov/omhd/About/disparities.htm (Accessed November 12, 2007).

Centers for Medicare & Medicaid Services. "CMS History Project—President's Speeches," undated, http://www.cms.hhs.gov/History/Downloads/CMSPresidentsSpeeches.pdf (Accessed May 9, 2007).

Cohn, Jonathan. *Sick: The Untold Story of America's Health Care Crisis—And the People Who Pay the Price.* New York: HarperCollins Publishers, 2007.

Collins, Sara R., et al. "On the Edge: Low-Wage Workers and Their Health Insurance Coverage." Commonwealth Fund Issue Brief, April 2003. http://www.commonwealthfund.org/usr_doc/collins_ontheedge_ib_626.pdf (Accessed May 15, 2007).

Commonwealth Fund Commission on a High Performance Health System. "Why Not the Best? Results from a National Scorecard on U.S. Health System Performance." 2006. http://www.commonwealthfund.org/usr_doc/Commission_whynotthebest_951.pdf (Accessed September 27, 2007).

Congressional Budget Office. "The State Children's Health Insurance Program." May 2007. http://www.cbo.gov/ftpdocs/80xx/doc8092/05-10-SCHIP.pdf (Accessed June 25, 2007).

Cutler, David M. *Your Money or Your Life: Strong Medicine for America's Health Care System.* New York: Oxford University Press, 2004.

Dobbin, Frank R. "The Origins of Private Social Insurance: Public Policy and Fringe Benefits in America, 1920–1950," *American Journal of Sociology,* March 1992, pp. 1416–1450 (Accessed through *JSTOR,* May 7, 2007).

Dorsey, Joseph L. "The Health Maintenance Organization Act

Bibliography

of 1973 (P.L. 93–222) and Prepaid Group Practice Plans." *Medical Care*, January 1975, p. 1.

Embry Thompson, Leah D., and Robert K. Kolbe. "Federal Tax Exemption of Prepaid Health Care Plans after IRC 501(M)," 1992. http://www.irs.gov/pub/irs-tege/eotopic 192.pdf (Accessed May 8, 2007).

Engel, Jonathan. *Doctors and Reformers: Discussion and Debate over Health Policy, 1925–1950*. Columbia: University of South Carolina Press, 2002.

Families USA. "President's Proposal Would Make Health Care Less, Not More, Affordable." Press release, February 15, 2006. http://www.familiesusa.org/resources/newsroom/statements/2007-statements/Presidents-Proposal-Would-Make.html (Accessed June 4, 2007).

Finkelstein, Amy. "The Cost of Coverage." *Wall Street Journal*, February 28, 2007, p. A14.

Funigiello, Philip J. *Chronic Politics: Health Care Security from FDR to George W. Bush*. Lawrence: University Press of Kansas, 2005.

Geyman, John. *Falling Through the Safety Net: Americans without Health Insurance*. Monroe, ME: Common Courage Press, 2005.

Goodman, John C., et al. *Lives at Risk: Single-Payer National Health Insurance around the World*. Lanham, MD: Rowman & Littlefield, 2004.

Graves, John A., and Sharon K. Long. "Why Do People Lack Health Insurance?" Urban Institute, May 22, 2006. http://www.urban.org/UploadedPDF/411317_lack_health_ins.pdf (Accessed May 15, 2007).

Gunnar, William P. "The Fundamental Law That Shapes the United States Health Care System: Is Universal Health Care Realistic Within the Established Paradigm?" *Annals of Health Law*, Winter 2006, p. 151.

Hacker, Jacob S. *The Great Risk Shift: The Assault on American Jobs, Families, Health Care, and Retirement and How You Can Fight Back*. New York: Oxford University Press, 2006.

Hacker, Jacob S. "Health Care for America." January 11, 2007. http://www.sharedprosperity.org/bp180/bp180.pdf (Accessed June 22, 2007).

Hadley, Jack, and John Holahan. "The Cost of Care for the Uninsured: What Do We Pay, Who Pays, and What Would Full Coverage Add to Medical Spending?" Kaiser Commission on Medicaid and the Uninsured, 2004, http://www.kff.org/uninsured/upload/The-Cost-of-Care-for-the-Uninsured-What-Do-We-Spend-Who-Pays-and-What-Would-Full-Coverage-Add-to-Medical-Spending.pdf (Accessed June 19, 2007).

Hale, R. W. "Legal Issues Impacting Women's Access to Care in the United States—The Malpractice Insurance Crisis." *International Journal of Gynecology & Obstetrics*, September 2006, p. 382.

Harding, T. Swann. "Our American System of State Medicine." *American Sociological Review*, December 1937, p. 875 (Accessed through JSTOR, May 24, 2007).

"Health Care: Time for Universal Coverage?" *Wall Street Journal*, June 2, 2007, p. A9.

Henley, Eric. "Malpractice Crisis: Causes of Escalating Insurance Premiums, and Implications for You." *Journal of Family Practice*, August 2006, p. 703.

Hill, J. Edward. "Ethical Issues in Health Care: Communicating and Persuading and Training." *Vital Speeches of the Day*, March 2007, p. 127.

Institute of Medicine. *Insuring America's Health: Principles and Recommendations*. Washington, DC: National Academies Press, 2004.

Bibliography

James, Cara, et al. "Key Facts: Race, Ethnicity, and Medical Care," Kaiser Family Foundation, January 2007. http://www.kff.org/minorityhealth/upload/6069-02.pdf (Accessed June 29, 2007).

Jonas, Steven. *An Introduction to the U.S. Health Care System*. 5th ed. New York: Springer, 2003.

Hadley, Jack, and John Holahan. "The Cost of Care for the Uninsured: What Do We Pay, Who Pays, and What Would Full Coverage Add to Medical Spending?" Kaiser Commission on Medicaid and the Uninsured, 2004. http://www.kff.org/uninsured/upload/The-Cost-of-Care-for-the-Uninsured-What-Do-We-Spend-Who-Pays-and-What-Would-Full-Coverage-Add-to-Medical-Spending.pdf (Accessed June 19, 2007).

Kaiser Family Foundation. "Election 2008: Health Advocacy Groups Partner to Promote Universal Health Insurance in Presidential Election," May 21, 2007, http://www.kaisernetwork.org/Daily_reports/rep_index.cfm?DR_ID=45039 (Accessed June 19, 2007).

Kaiser Family Foundation. "Health Insurance Premium Growth Moderates Slightly in 2006, But Still Increases Twice as Fast as Wages and Inflation." September 26, 2006. http://www.kff.org/insurance/ehbs092606nr.cfm (Accessed November 12, 2007).

Kershaw, Sarah, et al. "Eight States To Press Bush on Insurance Coverage of Children." *New York Times*, October 2, 2007, p. B1.

Kingson, Eric R., and John M. Cornman. "Health Care Reform: Universal Access Is Feasible and Necessary." *Benefits Quarterly*, Third Quarter 2007, p. 27.

Lueck, Sally. "Opening Bid on Health Care; Edwards's Plan for Universal Coverage to Be Matched by Rivals," *Wall Street Journal*, February 6, 2007, p. A4.

National Health Care

Lundberg, George D., and James Stacey. *Severed Trust: Why American Medicine Hasn't Been Fixed*. New York: Basic Books, 2000.

Malcomson, James M. "Health Service Gatekeepers." *Rand Journal of Economics*, Summer 2004, p. 401.

Markovchick, Vince. "'The Perfect Storm'—The Current Crisis State of U.S. Health Care." Speech presented at Cleveland State University, Cleveland-Marshall College of Law, Cleveland, Ohio. November 8, 2007.

Marmor, Theodore. "The Politics of Universal Health Insurance: Lessons from Past Administrations?" *PS: Political Science and Politics*, June 1994, p. 194.

McKinnon, John D., and Sarah Lueck. "Bush Bashes Democrats on Health; Differences over Funding of Insurance for Children Preview 2008 Battleground." *Wall Street Journal*, September 21, 2007, p. A9.

McLaughlin, Catherine G., ed. *Health Policy and the Uninsured*. Washington, DC: Urban Institute Press, 2004.

Mechanic, David. *The Truth about Health Care: Why Reform Is Not Working in America*. New Brunswick, NJ: Rutgers University Press, 2006.

Medical Care for the American People: The Final Report of the Committee on the Costs of Medical Care. Chicago: University of Chicago Press, 1932; reprinted Washington, D.C.: U.S. Department of Health, Education, and Welfare, 1970.

Mueller, Rudolph. *As Sick as It Gets: The Shocking Reality of America's Healthcare*. Dunkirk, NY: Olin Frederick, 2001.

Organisation for Economic Co-Operation and Development. *Health at a Glance 2007*. Paris: OECD, 2007.

PBS, "Healthcare Crisis: Who's at Risk? Program Transcript,"

Bibliography

2000. http://www.pbs.org/healthcarecrisis/transcript.html (Accessed May 2, 2007).

Pipes, Sally. *Miracle Cure: How to Solve America's Health Care Crisis and Why Canada Isn't the Answer.* San Francisco: Pacific Research Institute, 2004.

Pollack, Ron. "At the Hearing on H.R. 2355, the Health Care Choice Act," June 28, 2005. http://www.familiesusa.org/resources/newsroom/ron-pollack-testimony-health-care-choice-act.html (Accessed June 4, 2007).

Quadagno, Jill. *One Nation Uninsured: Why the U.S. Has No National Health Insurance.* New York: Oxford University Press, 2005.

Richmond, Julius B., and Rashi Fein. *The Health Care Mess: How We Got into It and What It Will Take to Get Out.* Cambridge, MA: Harvard University Press, 2005.

Rosenbaum, Sara, and Joel Teitelbaum. "Addressing Racial Inequality in Health Care." May 25, 2005. http://www.rwjf.org/files/research/135-Part%202-Chapter%209.pdf (Accessed June 29, 2007).

Sered, Susan Starr, and Rushika Fernandopulle. *Uninsured in America: Life & Death in the Land of Opportunity.* Berkeley: University of California Press, 2005.

Shapiro, Robert. "Premium Blend: Why Is It So Difficult To Provide Universal Health Care?" *Slate*, May 15, 2003. http://www.slate.com/id/2082988/ (Accessed June 24, 2007).

Smith, Vernon, et al. "SCHIP Turns 10: An Update on Enrollment and the Outlook on Reauthorization from the Program's Directors," Kaiser Commission on Medicaid and the Uninsured," May 2007. http://www.kff.org/medicaid/upload/7642.pdf (Accessed June 25, 2007).

Social Security Administration. "Chronology of Significant

Events Leading to Enactment of Medicare," undated, http://www.ssa.gov/history/cornignappa.html (Accessed May 8, 2007).

Sowada, Barbara J. *A Call To Be Whole: The Fundamentals of Health Care Reform.* Westport, CT: Praeger, 2003.

Syed, Athar H. *Health Care Crisis in America: A Cure.* Bangor, ME: Booklocker.com, Inc., 2005.

Tanner, Michael D., and Michael F. Cannon. "Universal Healthcare's Dirty Little Secrets." Cato Institute. April 2007. http://www.cato.org/pub_display.php?pub_id=8172 (Accessed June 24, 2007).

Terris, Milton. "National Health Insurance in the United States: A Drama in Too Many Acts," *Journal of Public Health Policy*, 1999, pp. 13–35 (Accessed through JSTOR, May 7, 2007).

U.S. Census Bureau, Current Population Reports, P60–233. *Income, Poverty, and Health Insurance Coverage in the United States: 2006* (Washington, DC: Government Printing Office, 2007). http://www.census.gov/prod/2007pubs/p60-233.pdf (Accessed September 27, 2007).

Walker, Forrest A. "Compulsory Health Insurance: 'The Next Great Step in Social Legislation.'" *Journal of American History*, September 1969, pp. 290–304. (Accessed through JSTOR, May 7, 2007).

Walker, David M. "America in 2017: Making Tough Choices Today Can Help Save Our Future." January 26, 2007. http://www.gao.gov/htext/d07417cg.html (Accessed May 7, 2007).

Index

Page numbers in **boldface** are illustrations, tables, and charts.

Access TN, 19
access to care, 90, 96–97, 99–100
Aetna Health Inc. v. Davila, 104
African Americans, 87, 112–114, **113**
age groups, 21, 34, 92, **94**
Alzheimer's Association, 83
Alzheimer's disease, 27
American Association for Justice, 111
American Association for Labor Legislation (AALL), 45,54
American Association for Retired Persons (AARP), 28, 54, 83
American Bar Association Standing Committee on Medical Professional Liability, 104
American Cancer Society Cancer Action Network, 83
American Diabetes Association, 83
American Federation of Labor (AFL), 45, 54
American Heart Association, 83
American Hospital Association, 47–48
American Medical Association (AMA), 39, 45–50, 54, 76, 95, 105, 107, 108–110
American Telephone and Telegraph (AT&T), 40
American Tort Reform Association, 108
asthma, 24, 28, **37**, 79, 98

back pain, 102–103
Back Pain Recognition Program, 102
Barton, Bob, 8
Baylor University, 47
Better Health Care Together
B. F. Goodrich Company, 45
binding fee schedule, 94

National Health Care

Blue Cross Blue Shield, 8, 17, 48
Blumenthal, Richard, 104–105
brand-name drugs, 30
Bush, George H. W., 58–59
Bush, George W., 17, **31**, 69, 70–71, 75, 76, 110, **115**

California, crisis in, 20–21, **84**
California Nurses Association, **84**
Campaign for America's Future, 86, 88
Canada's health system, 92, 96, 97
cancer, 23, 26–27, 79, 87, 98, 103, 120
capitalism, 63–64, 97
capitation, 105
cardiovascular disease, 23, 25, 27, 112–113, 120
Carter, Jimmy, 58
catastrophic events, 10, 19, 58
Cato Institute, 66, 77
Center for American Progress (CAP), 39–40, 89–90, 105, 119
Center for Studying Health System Change, 39
Center on Budget and Policy Priorities (CBPP), 81–82
Centers for Disease Control and Prevention (CDC), 87
Century Foundation, 71
charity care, 13, 15, 88
chemotherapy, 27
children's insurance, 81–82

low income, 51, 54–55, 58, 112, 114–116, **115**
cholesterol levels, 25, 28
chronic conditions, 23–26, 72
claims procedures, 11
Cleveland Clinic system, 15
Clinton, Bill, 34, 59–61, **60**, 114
Clinton, Hillary, 59, **60**, 117
Clinton plan, 59–62, **60**, 88, 114
Cohn, Jonathan, 87–88
Committee on Economic Security, 47
Committee on the Costs of Medical Care (CCMC), 46, 47
Commonwealth Fund, 16
competition, 40–41, 56
  free market, 63, 66–68, 78, 80, 82, 83, 97–98
  international, 87
Comprehensive Health Insurance Program, 57
computerized tomography (CT), 7, 27, 102
Congressional Budget Office, 109
Connecticut Association of Health Plans, 105
consumer protection, 78–79
Conyers, John, 91
copayment, 12, 16, 19, 40, 66, 76, 91
costs of medical care, **6**, 12–13
coverage limits, 19
Cover TN program, 19

Daschle, Tom, 39, 87, 98

Index

Davenport, Karen, 90, 105
Declaration of
 Independence, 111
deductibles, 12, 16, 19, 30,
 40, 66, 80, 96
 for HSAs, 68, 69, 70, 71,
 72
 tax reform and, 76
defensive medicine, 109
delayed care, 65–66, 97–98
DeMint, Jim, 78
denials of care/coverage,
 103–106
dental programs, 40, 91
Department of Health and
 Human Services, 17
Department of Veterans
 Affairs, 11
dependent-care benefits, 40
diabetes, 24, 78, 87, 120
diagnostic testing, 23, 59,
 109
 cost of, 6, 65
DirigoChoice program, 17
disability payments, 50, 55
doctors, 26, 59
 conflicts-of-interest, 105
 cost of training, 42, 44,
 64
"donut hole," 31
Dupuytren's contracture, 8

earned income credit, 77
Economic Policy Institute,
 88
Edwards, John, 117
elderly, 58, 95, 98, 103
 Medicare and, 51, **51**, 54,
 88–89
emergency care, 13, 59,
 85–86, 91
Emergency Medical
 Treatment and Active Labor
 Act (1986), 85
emergency rooms, **37**, **94**,
 100
 delayed care and, 65–66
employee cost share, 39, 40
 health care choice, 66–67,
 105
employer-provided
 insurance, 9–10, 16, 49,
 57, 66–67, 81
 California plans, 20–21
 under health security
 plan, 59–62
 HSAs and, 68, 119
 premiums, 16, 36, 38–40,
 66, 68, 76
 reduction/coverage loss,
 33–38
 self-funded plans, 77
 tax laws and, 74–77
 universal health care and,
 87, 88–89, 92, 117,
 118
Employment Retirement
 Income Security Act
 (ERISA), 58, 67, 104,
 105
entitlement programs, 54
ethnic inequality, 112–114,
 119
exclusions to coverage, 12,
 16–17, 92
eye care, 40, 91

Facchino, Alicia, 7–8, 13
Fair Share Health Care Fund
 Act, 19

Families USA, 28, 71, 76, 78
Fishbein, Morris, 47, 50
Flexner, Abraham, 42, 44
Food and Drug Administration, 29
Ford, Gerald, 58
for profit (private) hospitals, 13, 15, 91–92. *See also* private hospitals.
Freedom of Information Act, 93
free market competition, 63, 66–68, 78, 80, 82–83, 97–98
frivolous lawsuits, 110–111

Gabel, Jon, 39
"gag clauses," 105
Garfield, Sidney, 48
gatekeepers, 102
General Accounting Office, 72
generic drugs, 30
Giuliani, Rudy, 119
Gompers, Samuel, 45
government-funded health programs, 11, 40
  historically, 45, 54, 57, 60–61
  internationally, 40, 44
  SCHIP, 114–116, **115**
government regulation, 46–47, 61, 63, 78–79, 83, 95
Great Britain's system, 96, 97, 100
Great Depression, 46
gross domestic product (GDP), 15

group insurance, 36, 38, 48–49, 89
historic demand for, 45, 46, 57

Hacker, Jacob, 87, 88
health, factors influencing, 86–87, 120
Health Care Choice Act, 78
health care jobs, 64, **64**
Health Insurance Association of America, 61
health insurance exchanges, 79–82
Health Insurance Portability and Accountability Act (1996), 33
health insurance system, 9–17
  higher premiums/less coverage, 38–41
  reduction/loss of coverage, 33–38
health insurance exchanges, 79–82
health maintenance organization (HMO), 11, 48, 55–56, 59, 103
  employer contracts, 9–10, 104–105
Health Maintenance Organization Act (1973), 55
health savings accounts (HSAs), 68–74, 119
health security plan, 59–62, 60
health tax, 91

154

Index

Healthy-Adjusted Life Expectancy (HALE), 15
Heritage Foundation, 76, 78–82, 89
Hickey, Roger, 86, 89, 97
high-deductible plans, 21
high-risk procedures, 110
Hill, J. Edward, 39, 95
Hill-Burton Hospital Survey and Construction Act (1946), 50
hip replacement, 97, 99
HIV, 26
hospital care, 59, 65. *See also* for-profit (private) hospitals and non-profit (public) hospitals.
  cost of average stay, 26, 95
  prepayment, 47
House Committee on Energy and Commerce, 78
hypertension, 25, 120

infant mortality rate, 15, 87
insulin, 24
insurance companies, 67, 77–78, 93
  Clinton plan and, 61–62
  denial of coverage, 103–106
  types of contracts, 9–11, 36
  universal health care, 93, 117
insurance market, nationwide, 77–79
Intel, 40

Internal Revenue Service (IRS), 36, 48, 61, 75
international basic care, 90
  access to, 96–97, 99, 100
Internet pharmacies, 28, 30

JAMA, 47
job benefits, 36, 40, 94, 97
job security, 35, 87
  coverage and, 33–35, 81, 92
Johnson, Lyndon Baines, 50–51, **51**, 54

Kaiser Family Foundation, 39, 48, 109
Kelly, Thomas C., 85
Kelly Services, 40, 41
Kennedy, D. R., 45
Kennedy, Edward, 57, 58
Kerry, John, 88
King, Meredith, 114, 119
Kucinich, Dennis, 87, 91
Kuehl, Sheila James, 20

Lavizzo-Mourey, Risa, 85
lawsuits, 107–108, 110–111
Liberty Mutual Group, 103
life expectancy, 23–26, **24**
long-term care, 54, 91
low-income care, 13, 18, 57, 81–82, 87, 89, 112
  children, 51, 54–55, 58, 81–82, 112, 114–116, **115**

magnetic resonance imaging (MRI), 27
Maine programs, 17

malpractice, 28, 58, 106–111, **107**, 119
malpractice insurance, 13, 108–111
managed care, 11, 59–60, 101–102
  criticisms, 103–106
  pluses, 102–103
mandatory participation, 83, 117, 119
marginal tax rate, 75, 76
market-based reform, 63, 98, 119
Maryland programs, 19
Massachusetts' Connector program, 18, 80, 82
Massachusetts' programs, 17, 18
maternity care, 79
McCain, John, 119
McMasters, Frank, 27
Medicaid, 11, 18, **18**, 54–55, 57, 60–61, 81, 85, 88, 114, 117
medical schools, 44
Medicare, 11, **14**, 50–51, **51**, 54–55
  health care costs under, 13, 57, 60–61, 119
  Part A, 54
  Part B, 54
  Part D, 31, 32, 33
  prescription drug program, 31-33, **31**
  universal health care and, 85, 88–89, 91, 95
Medicare-plus plan, 88–89
mental health, 59, 79, 91, 120

MetroHealth System, 15
Milken Institute, 120
Moore, Michael, 91, 95
Mountain States Health Alliance, 19
Moynihan, Patrick, 61
multiple sclerosis, 7–8, 26
muscular dystrophy, 26

National Academy of Sciences Institute of Medicine, 83–84, 85
National Center for Policy Analysis, 78
National Committee for Quality Assurance (NCQA), 102
national health insurance. *See* Universal health care.
National Health Insurance Standards Act, 56–57
National Health Plan, 58
needle fasciotomy, 8
network of doctors, 11
Nixon, Richard, 55–58
nonprofit (public) hospitals, 15, 91.
  See also public hospitals.
  emergency care, 13, 66
Núñez, Fabian, 21

Obama, Barack, 117, **118**
obesity, 15, 119
obstetricians/gynecologists (OBGYN), 109, 110
Organization for Economic Co-Operation and Development (OECD), 14, 15, 27, 93

Index

Pacific Research Institute, 95
pain management, 102
part-time/full-time workers, 36
patent protection, 29
patient bill of rights, 105
patient liability, 12
payment, 88–90
   one payer, 90–95
   private-public, 88–90, 96
pension plans, 40, 54, 58
Perata, Don, 21
personal choice, influencing health, 86, 87
"personal responsibility" programs, 17–18
Pharmaceutical Research and Manufacturers of America (PhRMA), 29
Physicians for a National Health Program, 91
plaintiff, 106
Pollack, Ron, 71, 76
positron-emission tomography (PET), 27
preapproval policies, 11
preexisting conditions, 12, 21, 34, 36, 59, 94, 117
premiums, 9–10, 16, 36, 49, 58, 60–61, 76
   for HSAs, 71
   increasing, 38–40, 74, 83, 106
   for malpractice, 108–111
   state plans and, 17, 79, 80
prepayment, 47, 48, 49
prescription drugs, 18, 30–31, **43**, 103
   costs of, 23–25, **25**, 28–33, 91

presidential candidate plans, 117–119, **118**
preventive care, 50, 55, 59, 69, 117, 120
price inflation, 55
price sensitivity, 65–66, 69
primary care, 11, 102
Prince George's Hospital, 15
private hospitals, 13, 15, **37**
   See also for-profit-hospitals.
   universal health care and, 91–92
private insurance plan, 10–11, 13, 20, 49, 68, 76, 88–90, 92, 96–97, 117, **118**
   Part D coverage and, 31–33
profit motive, 106, 109
Progressive Party, 44
Projan, Steven, 29
Public Citizen, 91
public health care plans, 88–90, 96, 117, **118**
public hospitals, 13, 15, 20, **37**, 92.
See also non-profit hospitals.
public/private plans, 88–90, 96, 117, **118**

quality of care, 103–104, **107**, 109
   racial/ethnic inequality, 112–114, **113**

racial differences, influencing health, 87, 112, **113**

157

National Health Care

radiation therapy, 26
rationing, 96–98, 100, 101
Reagan, Ronald, 58
referrals, 11, 102
regulation
 federal, 29, 78
 tate, 48, 55, 77, 79, 80
reinsurance, 88
rescue medicine, 25
research and development, 29, 94
resistance to change, 114–117, 119
risk pools, 78
Robert Wood Johnson Foundation, 85
Romney, Mitt, 119
Roosevelt, Franklin D., 47
Roosevelt, Theodore, 44, 45, 120

Schwarzenegger, Arnold, 20–21, 93, **94**
Scott, Lee, 40
Scully, Tom, 89
second opinion, 102
self-insured plans, 10–11, 36, 46, 57–58, 60, 70, 77, 89
Senate Bill 840 (California), 20
Seshamani, Meena, 40
Shadegg, John, 78
single-payer system, 90–95, 96
skilled nursing facility, 54
Smith, Adam, 63
Snow, John, 70, **70**
socialized medicine, 50, 53, 93
Social Security, 36, 47, 54

socioeconomic factors, influencing health, 86–87, 112
special interest groups, 54
specialists, 11, 93, 100, 102
 malpractice insurance, 109–110
Spitzer, Eliot, 103
Stabenow, Debbie, 32
"standard of care," 8, 82
State Children's Health Insurance Program (SCHIP), 114–117, **115**
state programs, 17, 19
 discount drug program, **25**
 health care reform plans, 17–19
 health insurance exchanges, 79–82
 Medicaid programs, 55
 regulation, 48, 55, 77, 79
 SCHIP, 114–116, 117
 tort laws, 104–105, 109, 110–111
stents, 27
stop-loss policy, 10
substance abuse programs, 59, 91
surgery costs, 11, 26, 65

Taft, William Howard, 44, 45
Target, generic drug plan, 30
taxation, 46–47, 50, 57, 61, 75, 91, 95, 117, **118**
 deductions, 75–76
 exemptions, 9–10, 13, 48–49, 66, 69, **70**, 74, 76
 penalties, 18, 20–21

Index

tax credit, 76–77, 89–90, 119
technology, cost of new, **6**, 26–28, 65, 94, 109
Tennessee programs, 19
tort laws, 104–105, 109, 110–111
Truman, Harry S., 49–50, 52–53, 54

umbrella organizations, 15, 19
underinsured, 16, 83, 95, 96, 98
uninsured, 8–9, 16–17, 76, 83, 98
   children, 114–116, **115**
   health care costs, **6**, 7–9, 13, 15, 30–31, 39, 95
   job change and, 33–35, 81, 86, 92
unions, 40–41, 49, 54, 57–58
United States
   health care costs in, **56**, 100
   health system ranking, 15, 16
U.S. Constitution, 84–85, 111
U.S. Supreme Court, 104
universal health care, 19, 52–53, 57, 83–100, **84**, 101
   Clinton plan, 61
   opponents to, 45–47, 94–100
   payment plans for, 88–95, 96
   presidential candidates' plans,

117–119, **118**
   supporters, 84–88, 93, 95–96, 99
   Truman 5-point plan, 50, 52–53
University Hospital system, 15
unnecessary procedures, 11, 102

value-added tax (VAT), 90
Vermont programs, 17
Veterans Administration, 32

Wal-Mart, 19, 30, 36, 40
"war on poverty," 51
Waxman, Senator Henry, 29–30
Wilson, Woodrow, 45
workers' compensation, 36
World Health Organization, 16
World War I, 45
World War II, 48, 49
Wyeth Pharmaceuticals, 29

x-ray, **6**, 7, 102

About the Author

Kathiann M. Kowalski has written twenty books and more than 450 articles and stories for young people. Kowalski received her bachelor's degree in political science from Hofstra University and her law degree from Harvard Law School, where she was an editor of the *Harvard Law Review*. Kowalski has spent more than twenty years practicing law and writing books. Her books have won awards from the Society of School Librarians International, the American Society for the Prevention of Cruelty to Animals, the National Science Teachers Association and the Children's Book Council, and The Pennsylvania School Librarians Association (PSLA). Her most recent book in this series was *Free Trade*.

```
HMNTW 362
       .1
       K88
```

KOWALSKI, KATHIANN M.
   NATIONAL HEALTH CARE

MONTROSE
04/09